Harper was pregnant?

Jack let the words sink into his brain. She was having a baby. A sharp prick of disappointment stabbed him in the gut. Harper was having someone else's baby. Not that he was keen on having a family or anything himself, but still... She had moved on and found someone else and got pregnant. But what did that news have to do with him? She didn't look like she was very far along. Was she in the early stages? He knew that pregnancy could trigger appalling nausea in some women that required hospital admission. Why, then, had she called him? He wasn't her next of kin, he wasn't her partner—he wasn't, strictly speaking, even a friend. It didn't make sense. She had friends and family, surely? And what about her partner, the father of her baby? That was who was supposed to be by her side right now. Not him. A casual lover she had cast off without a backward glance.

"Are you the proud father?" the nurse asked Jack with a beaming smile.

"No, I—"

"Yes," Harper said. "He's the father."

Weddings Worth Billions

Say yes...to the wedding of your dreams!

At Happily Ever After Weddings, nothing short of perfection will do! Best friends Ruby, Harper and Aerin will not rest until they give each überrich client a wedding beyond their wildest dreams.

Still, while the trio witness true love on an almost daily basis, they have yet to experience it themselves. Will the arrival of three billionaires lead Ruby, Harper and Aerin to say "I do," too?

Read Ruby and Lucas's story in
Cinderella's Invitation to Greece

Read Harper and Jack's story in
Nine Months After That Night

Both available now!

Catch Aerin's story coming soon!

Melanie Milburne

———

NINE MONTHS AFTER THAT NIGHT

ISBN-13: 978-1-335-73882-0

Nine Months After That Night

Copyright © 2022 by Melanie Milburne

Harlequin Enterprises ULC
22 Adelaide St. West, 41st Floor
Toronto, Ontario M5H 4E3, Canada
www.Harlequin.com

Printed in U.S.A.

Melanie Milburne read her first Harlequin novel at the age of seventeen, in between studying for her final exams. After completing a master's degree in education, she decided to write a novel, and thus her career as a romance author was born. Melanie is an ambassador for the Australian Childhood Foundation and a keen dog lover and trainer. She enjoys long walks in the Tasmanian bush. In 2015 Melanie won the HOLT Medallion, a prestigious award honoring outstanding literary talent.

Books by Melanie Milburne

Harlequin Presents

The Billion-Dollar Bride Hunt

Once Upon a Temptation

His Innocent's Passionate Awakening

The Scandalous Campbell Sisters

Shy Innocent in the Spotlight
A Contract for His Runaway Bride

Wanted: A Billionaire

One Night on the Virgin's Terms
Breaking the Playboy's Rules
One Hot New York Night

Weddings Worth Billions

Cinderella's Invitation to Greece

Visit the Author Profile page
at Harlequin.com for more titles.

To my beautiful grandchildren Willow Esme and Torrance Theodore. You have blessed my life in so many ways and brought such joy and laughter. It will be a long time before you can read Nanny's books, but this one is dedicated to you all the same. xxxxxx

CHAPTER ONE

HARPER LAY ON the hospital gurney in a sweat-soaked panic. Was she going to die? The niggling pain in her back that had started three days ago was getting worse. It was spreading to her abdomen—tight, rigid bands that made it hard for her to breathe. Was it endometriosis? Or…or *cancer*? She was only twenty-seven—how could she die of cancer? She had so much left to do. Her career was taking off. She had a book deal featuring her photographs—photographs she had yet to take in Paris in six weeks' time. This was definitely the wrong time to contract a terminal illness.

The pain gradually subsided like a retreating tide and Harper flopped back on the pillow and let out a shuddering breath. But she knew it would be back. The time intervals between the spasms were shrinking.

Only a junior doctor had examined her so far and he had seemed a little baffled by Harper's symptoms. The doctor took a blood sample for Pathology and told Harper the more senior emergency doctor would be back with the results, as soon as they came through.

Harper closed her eyes and tried to meditate while she waited for the results of the test. Not that meditation had ever been her forte. Her one and only visit to a health spa retreat had made her feel antsy and agitated the whole time, while everyone else was chanting and cleansing and rebalancing their chakras. Her chakras were obviously beyond repair. As for her mind? It was hardly ever still, which she put down to her turbulent childhood. All that time in foster care had made her hypervigilant. Every noise, every sound, every footfall and she was wide awake and alert.

A and E was busy with the usual dramas of a Saturday night. Harper could hear the noise of someone coughing a couple of cubicles away. Not a simple virus cough but one that hinted at some sort of hideous lung disease like emphysema or cancer.

Cancer.

Why could she not stop thinking about the C word?

A man was shouting in another cubicle about wanting more morphine. Harper wondered if he was suffering from the same disease. Maybe the Swan women weren't destined to live beyond thirty. Her mother had died young, so too her grandmother.

Another band of pain tightened around her abdomen like an iron cable. Sweat poured like tears from her hairline, her teeth were gritted together so hard she was sure she was going to crack every one of her molars. But hey, if she was going to die, what would it matter if every tooth fell out?

I don't want to die!

It was a scream inside her brain, as if a panic button had been pressed in her head, a piercing siren of distress only she could hear.

The curtain was swished aside and a more senior emergency doctor came in. She placed a hand on Harper's wrist, her expression grave. 'Is your partner waiting outside?'

'I don't have a partner.'

'Oh, well, your next of kin? Your mother?'

'My mother died when I was eight.' Harper could say it without any trace of emotion but it had taken years of practice. Years of concealing her true feelings behind a mask of indifference. Years of blocking the vision of finding her mother lying lifeless on the floor of their cramped bedsit when she came home from school on that fateful day. Later than she should have come home. If she hadn't stopped on the walk home to play with a stray kitten...

'A sibling?'

'I'm an only child.' Which, strictly speaking wasn't quite true. Harper had several half-siblings she had never met because her father hadn't wanted his dirty little secret—*her*, his secret love child—to be revealed to his wife and family. 'Love child' was a bit of a stretch. Her father hadn't loved Harper's mother. He had used her to break his marital boredom and then left her when she got pregnant.

'Harper…' The female doctor's voice was gentle, as if she was preparing to deliver shocking news.

'It's okay, Dr Praneesh,' Harper said with a grim smile. 'You can be straight with me. It's cancer, isn't it?'

Dr Praneesh frowned. 'No, you don't have cancer.' She moistened her lips and continued, 'It's a different type of growth—you're pregnant.'

Harper rapid-blinked. Her heart knocked against her ribcage with the force of a punch. 'I—I can't possibly be pregnant.' Was she having some sort of hallucination? A bad dream? How could she be pregnant and not know? And more to the point—*not show*? Sure, she wasn't the slimmest woman on the planet but she could distinguish a baby bump.

'When was the last time you had intercourse?'

'Erm…months ago.'

'Nine months?'

Harper did the mental arithmetic, a worm of worry wriggling through her mind. Her stomach swooped and dipped and dived. Her one-night stand with Jack Livingstone. How could she be pregnant to a playboy? It was her worst nightmare. How could she tell him? How could she rock up to him carrying a full-term baby in her arms? How could she be having Jack's baby? Anyone's baby? She hadn't planned on having kids. She wasn't the maternal type. She was a career woman. She had no room in her life for a baby. She hadn't even held a baby since she was a kid. 'Yes, but that's ridiculous. I—I've had a period every month since.' She looked down at her slightly rounded abdomen just as the pain began again. 'Oh, God, here it comes again.' She gripped the doctor's hand so hard Dr Praneesh winced.

'You're in labour, Harper. It seems you've had a cryptic pregnancy. It's not as rare as you'd think. One in two thousand five hundred pregnancies in the UK, which is about three hundred a year. You can still have a light period each month and not have any other symptoms of pregnancy, or at least none that you notice, especially if the placenta is in the front of the abdomen, as it lessens the sensations of the foetus kicking and moving. I'll have to examine you to see how close you are to delivering.'

'Delivering…' Harper swallowed a lump of dread. 'You mean, I'm having a baby? *Now?*' Her panicked shriek rivalled the volume of Morphine Man in cubicle six.

'Your contractions are ten minutes apart, so it won't be long now. From what you told the triage nurse, you've been in non-active labour a couple of days. I'll do an ultrasound to check the baby's development, and the sex if you'd like to know, and then do an internal examination. Would you like to call a friend or the baby's father to be with you?'

Harper gulped. Her two best friends and business partners were out of town—Ruby had only days ago got engaged to Lucas Rothwell and was spending the weekend with him in the Lake District. And Aerin was visiting her parents in Buckinghamshire for their thirty-sixth wedding anniversary. God only knew where Jack Livingstone would be—no doubt in bed with his latest hook-up in one of his plush hotels. But she had to tell him, right? He was the father and he had to be given the choice to be present at the baby's birth, not to mention the choice to be a part of his child's life.

Like her own father, he could always say no.

Jack was poring over some bookwork in his London penthouse at his boutique flagship hotel when his phone buzzed on his desk. He glanced at it and gave a slow smile when he saw who was calling him at this late hour on a Saturday night. Maybe the elusive Harper Swan had changed her mind and decided to see him again and collect the earring he still had in his possession. 'Hello there.'

He could hear her heavy breathing on the end of the line. 'Jack, there's no easy way to tell you this…but I'm in hospital and—'

Jack sat bolt upright in his chair, something in his chest flapping like a wind-whipped sail. 'Are you all right? What's wrong? Have you had an accident?'

'Kind of…' Harper gave an audible swallow. 'I'd like to explain in person…if that's okay? Are you in London right now?'

'I am.' He pushed back his chair and reached for his jacket and sports car keys. 'Which hospital are you in?'

'St Agnes's. I'm still in A and E but—'

'I'll be there in a few minutes.' Jack ended the call and then opened the second drawer in his desk. He took out the earring she had left behind after their one-night stand and slipped it into his pocket. At least now he would be able to give it to her in person.

Jack wasn't a fan of hospitals but something about Harper's call had set his nerves on edge. She had mentioned some sort of accident. A minor prang? A bump on the head? She must have a concussion if she'd changed her mind about seeing him. She had ignored his calls for months and, while he'd been disappointed, he hadn't let it get to him. He wasn't the type of man to get hung up on a woman. He had enjoyed their one night together and had hoped for a fling with her but she hadn't seemed interested in a follow-up. Harper had been so adamant about not seeing him again she had refused to collect her earring. He knew he could have posted it or dropped it off at her office but he had kept it. He couldn't explain why other than every time he looked at it, it reminded him of their explosive night of bed-wrecking, spine-tingling, mind-scrambling sex.

Jack also couldn't explain why he hadn't had a hook-up with anyone since. It was out of character for him to leave it so long but he'd been busy acquiring another property for development in Yorkshire. He hadn't wanted any distractions while he secured the Rothwell Park deal. Turning the ancient estate into one of his boutique hotels was a dream he had harboured for months and now it was coming to fruition. Not that reliving every second of that night of passion with Harper wasn't a distraction in itself. He had found it near impossible to get her out of his mind. Was it because she had walked away without begging for a follow-up date like every other woman he'd met? The challenge of winning Harper over was like a background thrum in his blood. He tried to ignore the niggling sense of failing at a goal he had set himself. A box that hadn't been ticked to his satisfaction. Not that he viewed any woman as a prize or trophy he could win, but because something about Harper got to him in a way no other woman ever had.

Once he arrived at the hospital, Jack was led by a nurse to the A and E cubicle Harper was in. 'Here she is.' The nurse gave a briskly efficient smile. 'We're waiting on an orderly to collect her. He shouldn't be too long now.'

Harper was lying on the hospital gurney on her side, her features pinched and white and racked with pain. Sweat poured down her face and in one of her hands she had a blue stress ball that she was squeezing so hard it was bulging in between her fingers like a squashed plum. But then a flood of colour entered her cheeks. 'Jack…' Her voice was a strangled whisper, her grey-green eyes not quite willing to meet his. 'I'm *so* sorry…'

Jack took her other hand and gave it a gentle squeeze. 'Hey, you. What's going on?'

'I don't know how to tell you this…' She bit her lip so hard he was worried it would split and bleed. 'I thought it was backache. I had no idea. I truly didn't. I didn't think it was possible to not know, to not recognise the signs. I didn't even *have* any signs that I can remember.'

'Signs? What are you talking about?'

'I thought it was cancer. Can you believe that?' She bit off a self-deprecating laugh and pulled her hand out of his and pushed her sweat-soaked hair back off her face. 'I thought the doctor was going to tell me I had inoperable cancer. That I was dying at the ripe old age of twenty-seven.'

A fist of fear clutched at Jack's guts. 'You don't have cancer…do you?'

'No…' She bit her lip again and squeezed the stress ball hard, her features contorting in pain. 'I feel so stupid. How am I going to explain this to everyone? To Aerin and Ruby? We have weddings booked solidly for the next two months, including Ruby's and Lucas's. Summer is our busiest time of year. I mean, it's like a bad dream or something. I can't believe this has happened to me of all people.'

The cubicle curtain was twitched aside and the nurse reappeared. 'The orderly is on his way now to take you to the maternity ward.'

Maternity ward? The words were like a bomb going off in Jack's head. *Ba-boom*. His thoughts flying everywhere like shrapnel. He whipped around so quickly to face the nurse he almost knocked over the portable blood pressure machine.

He reached out to steady it with a shaking hand. 'Maternity?' His voice came out hoarse, his heart thumping as if he needed to be admitted himself. To the cardiac unit.

'I was trying to tell you…' Harper said, with a frustrated eye-roll.

'Tell me what?'

'I'm having a baby.'

Harper was pregnant?

Jack let the words sink into his brain. She was having a baby. A sharp prick of disappointment stabbed him in the gut. Harper was having someone else's baby. Not that he was keen on having a family or anything himself, but still. She had moved on and found someone else and got pregnant. But what did that news have to do with him? She didn't look as if she was very far along. Was she in the early stages? He knew that pregnancy could trigger appalling nausea in some women that required hospital admission. Why, then, had she called him? He wasn't her next of kin, he wasn't her partner—he wasn't strictly speaking even a friend. It didn't make sense. She had friends and family, surely? And what about her partner, the father of her baby? That was who was supposed to be by her side right now. Not him. A casual lover she had cast off without a backward glance.

'Are you the proud father?' the nurse asked Jack with a beaming smile.

'No, I—'

'Yes,' Harper said. 'He's the father.'

Jack stared at Harper in a gobsmacked silence. How could he be the father? He hadn't seen Harper in months. Nine months. He had counted every one of them. He gave his head a shake, wondering if he was caught in some weird time warp. Nothing was making any sense. 'I'm the father? How?'

But there was no time for clarification or explanation, for the orderly came in with energetic efficiency and released the brake on the gurney.

'First baby?' the orderly said with a cheery smile.

'Yes…*oh*—' Harper's voice was cut off by a spasm of pain that flashed over her features.

Jack glanced at the nurse, who was collecting Harper's purse and phone from the table next to the gurney. 'Can't you give her something for the pain?'

'I don't want anything,' Harper said before the nurse could respond. 'I want a natural birth.'

Jack wasn't exactly up to date on what was de rigueur around pregnancy and motherhood these days but he had heard the term 'natural birth' bandied about and it sounded as if it could be extremely painful. 'This is the twenty-first century,

Harper,' Jack said, following alongside her as the orderly wheeled the gurney towards the lift situated outside A and E. 'There's no need to suffer unnecessarily.'

'I know, but I figure the only way I'll accept this is really happening to me is if I feel everything now.'

'You're not making a lot of sense. You've had nine months to prepare yourself.' Jack had had only minutes. It wasn't enough. His head was reeling, he was light-headed, his pulse was racing, his heart thumping with a host of emotions—panic, dread, fear. He was about to become a father. It didn't seem real. It didn't seem possible. They had used protection. He had never had a yearning desire to have children. He enjoyed his freedom too much. Why hadn't Harper told him before now? Why hadn't she given him the heads-up months ago? Or had she been worried he would pressure her to have a termination? He would not have done any such thing, but he would have liked to know he was to become a father well before the day of its freaking birth.

Never had he felt so out of control.

So blindsided.

It was like finding himself as a fully signed up member of a club he had never expected to join— the Fatherhood Club. Once in, you couldn't leave.

'I haven't had nine months to prepare,' Harper flashed back. 'I only just found out half an hour ago.'

'Cryptic pregnancy,' the orderly explained. 'It's not common but it happens. I've seen one before. Teenage girl had no idea she was pregnant until she got to A and E with severe abdominal pain. She thought it was appendicitis. You should have seen her mother's face when she was told she was about to become a grandmother.'

A cryptic pregnancy. So Harper hadn't known? How could she *not* have known? Surely there had been a hint or two? Or had she been so determined to put everything to do with him out of her mind she hadn't noticed the subtle changes in her body? But then, denial was a powerful mental tool. It could make normally rational and sensible people ignore things they didn't want to face. Issues they didn't want to deal with, truths they didn't want to confront.

There was an issue Jack had to face and fast. He was going to be a father and he wanted his child to have his name. Marrying had not been part of his life plan but he was going to have to rethink that, otherwise his child would grow up without the protection and shelter of being a Livingstone. Marriage was a monumental step for any couple but for him and Harper, who had only met once before—the night they conceived their baby—it was off-the-charts madness to be thinking about tying the knot. But marrying Harper and raising their child together was the only option. He couldn't see any other way forward. He had not had the happiest childhood himself due to his father's long and painful decline in health but that didn't mean Jack couldn't give his child a wonderful childhood. But he couldn't do it from a distance. He wanted to be a hands-on dad, involved from the get-go. Marrying Harper and providing a safe and secure home for their baby was the only thing he could control in this out-of-control situation.

The lift doors swished open. They all bundled inside and the doors closed again. Jack glanced at the sign reading Maternity Wing on the third floor and his guts turned to gravy. He glanced at Harper but she was in the middle of another savage contraction. Her face was screwed up, her panting breaths sounding as primal as those of a cavewoman. He took one of her hands and she gripped it until he thought his bones would snap like twigs. He figured now was probably not the best time to propose marriage.

'Are you sure you don't want some pain relief?' he asked with a concerned frown.

'If you can't stomach seeing me in pain, don't

come to the birth,' Harper said, through gritted teeth. 'No one's forcing you.'

'You want me to be there?'

'Only if you *want* to be there.' Her emphasis on the word 'want' didn't escape his notice.

Jack scraped his free hand through his hair. 'It's not something I've ever thought about before.' Like marriage, like commitment, like settling down with one person for the rest of his life. But he had a child to consider, a baby who was about to be born in the next few minutes. A baby he was not prepared for in any way.

The lift doors swished open on the maternity floor and his heart gave another almighty lurch.

'Better hurry and make up your mind, then,' Harper said on an expelled breath as strong as a wind gust. 'I have a feeling this baby isn't going to wait.'

CHAPTER TWO

HARPER WAS WHEELED into the delivery suite and she mentally prepared herself for Jack abandoning her at the door. But to her surprise he didn't. It was obvious he was way out of his depth suddenly finding himself smack bang in a maternity unit, but then, so was she. His features were white with shock, his stance stiff and guarded as if preparing himself for an event he had never expected to experience.

The birth of a child.

His child.

Her child.

Their child.

Harper was still having trouble getting her head around the fact she was about to deliver a baby. A baby her body had harboured in secret for close to nine months. A baby she had done nothing to prepare for—no clothes, no toys, no accessories, no pastel-painted nursery, no pram or baby seat or

changing table. She had done no emotional preparation, either. No sense of excitement or anticipation, so sense of joy or wonder. No connection with
the baby at all. Surely that was bad for the baby?
Would her baby sense her lack of preparation? Her
lack of anticipation and joy? Her lack of emotion?

Harper's decision to refuse pain relief was her
way of finally coming to terms with the reality of
what was happening. Otherwise, she was worried
she wouldn't properly bond with the baby. She
might not know much about babies but she did
know bonding was everything. Some of the kids
she had grown up with in foster care had not experienced secure bonding with their parents. Although on one level she knew her mother had loved
her, she still had reason to question her mother's
overall commitment to her. Her mother had always
seemed a little overwhelmed by being a single
parent—it hadn't been what she had been expecting, having loved Harper's father and dreamed of
them living happily ever after together. Harper had
put her mother's distant parenting style down to
the fact that her father had left her mother holding the baby, so to speak, not supporting her at
all, either financially or emotionally. That lack of
support had led to her mother ending her life, the
burden of bringing up a child alone too much for
her to handle.

Harper was determined not to repeat the cycle. She would do everything in her power to bond with her baby, to provide love and support no matter what.

Her baby.

The words were so foreign to her, like those of another language. The language of motherhood she hadn't planned on learning. Not for her talking to friends about sleep times and feeding schedules and babies' milestones. Not for her the endless hours of self-sacrifice and sleepless nights her mother had spoken of in one of her many down periods. Not for her the interruption of her much-loved career.

But those things were destined to be Harper's to experience now. She had no choice in the matter. Would she be a good mother? How would she juggle her career with an infant? There was so much to think about, to organise, and yet here she was, minutes away from holding her baby for the first time. But how was she supposed to bond with a baby she'd had no idea was coming? She hadn't stroked her abdomen for the last nine months, talking to her baby bump the way first-time mothers were encouraged to do. What if her lack of engagement with the baby so far caused irreparable damage? Panic swept through her in a flood as she suddenly realised she didn't have a name picked out. It wasn't something she had ever thought about—naming a child. She hadn't even named a pet, much less a child. The responsibility terrified her. What if her baby grew up hating the name she'd given her? What if it didn't suit the baby's personality? She tried to think of some names but her brain was sluggish with tiredness and pain, her thoughts as jumbled as clothes in a dryer that had overrun its cycle.

Harper glanced up at Jack, her heart thumping. 'We have to think of a name.'

'What, now?'

'We should have some names ready. One for a boy, one for a girl.'

'You don't know the sex?'

'No, when the doctor in A and E gave me an ultrasound, while I was waiting for you, I chose not to find out. I want it to be a surprise.'

His look was ironic, his tone dry. 'Haven't there been enough surprises already?'

'Good point.'

The midwife came in and introduced herself. 'My name is Meg. I'll be looking after you during the delivery. I need to examine you, if that's okay?'

'Do you want me to go out?' Jack asked.

'No,' Harper said, surprising herself. The thought of being so exposed and vulnerable with him watching should have embarrassed her, but she wanted his support. Needed it. It was too late to call any-one else…besides, she wanted her baby to meet its father. For him to be one of the first people to wel-come the baby into the world.

The midwife examined her while Jack held Harper's hand. He mopped the sweat from her brow with a soft cloth the midwife had handed him. Harper prepared herself for another contrac-tion, breathing into it, quietly amazed at the power of her body as it laboured to bring the baby further down the birth canal.

'You're just about fully dilated,' the midwife said, pulling the cover back over Harper's bent legs. 'Not long now.'

'Good, because this is getting pretty intense…' Harper clenched her teeth and squeezed Jack's hand.

'I'm going to check on a patient next door,' Meg said. 'Press the buzzer if anything changes.'

'Will do.'

'You're doing so well, Harper,' Jack said, once the midwife had gone.

'Names…' Harper said between panting breaths. 'We have to decide on a name…'

'Maybe we should wait until we meet the baby.'

'I want to have a name for my baby. I haven't got anything else ready, the least I can do is choose a name.' Tears formed in her eyes and she choked back a sob. What sort of mother was she going to be if she couldn't even think of a name for her baby?

Jack stroked the damp hair back from her forehead. 'Okay. Do you have any favourites?'

It was impossible to think clearly when her body was in the throes of another contraction. 'Not really, do you?'

He frowned in thought. 'I guess it would have to go with my name.'

Harper narrowed her gaze. 'Why's that?'

'I want the baby to have my surname.'

'Why?'

'Because we'll have to get married, that's why.'

Harper gaped at him. *'Married?'* She choked back a laugh of disbelief. 'You're surely not serious?'

'Of course I'm serious. I want to provide for my child and the best way to do that is for us to marry.'

Harper didn't get the chance to argue the point, for another contraction took hold as well as the overwhelming desire to push. 'Quick—press the buzzer for the midwife. I think the baby's coming.'

Jack reached for the buzzer and the midwife and her assistant came in soon after. He knew his job was to support Harper, so he concentrated on mopping her brow and holding her hand so she could ride out the final contractions. But it was agony to watch her, knowing it was his fault she was pregnant. How on earth had it happened? He was always so careful. He never had sex without protection. But somehow they had made a baby together and it was about to come into the world. He hadn't seen a birth before, only an acted one in a movie or television show. Nothing could have prepared him for the reality of childbirth. What a woman had to go through—the torturous pain, the indignity of having her body so open and exposed, the sheer vulnerability of giving birth astounded him. A flicker of fear lit in his gut and spread like a forest fire. What if things went wrong? Women still occasionally died from complications in childbirth and sometimes so did the baby. What if there was nothing he could do to save either of them? He was totally useless with his field of knowledge of hotel development. He knew little of medicine other than basic first aid. The sense of powerlessness sent his heart rate soaring and a trickle of sweat to drip down his spine.

'Time to push,' Meg the midwife said, coaching Harper in the final stages. 'Strip off your gown so we can put baby skin on skin. You too, Jack. Open your shirt so the baby can feel your skin and get to know your smell.'

Jack swallowed a boulder of emotion as he

helped Harper pull her gown down off her shoulders, before he undid his own shirt buttons. He wasn't the sort of guy to cry. He hadn't even cried at his father's funeral. But right then, a wave of unexpected emotion swept through him like a tsunami. His chest tightening as if his heart was looking for room to expand but held back by the cage of his ribs.

Harper gave a primal cry and bore down, her hand gripping his with pulverising force.

'You can do it, sweetie. Almost there,' he said, glancing at the business end of things where he could see a tiny dark-haired head crowning. It didn't seem real, it didn't seem possible he was glimpsing his own flesh and blood. His chest swelled, his heart thumped, his breath stalled at the raw and earthy beauty of seeing his baby come into the world.

Harper gave another cavewoman scream and the baby was expelled from her body. The midwife scooped the little wizened bundle up and laid it on Harper's naked chest, umbilical cord still attached. 'You have a beautiful daughter. Congratulations.'

He had a daughter. The baby gave a loud cry that to Jack was like the sweetest music he had ever heard. He blinked against the sting of tears, his throat so tight he couldn't speak. The rush of emotion at seeing his daughter for the first time blindsided him as much as Harper's cryptic pregnancy. The tiny body curled up like a comma on Harper's chest was *his* little girl.

His mother would be overjoyed. She had dropped hints for years about grandchildren but he'd always shut her down, telling her not to get her hopes up. Like him, his mother hadn't had time to prepare for such a momentous event but he knew she would relish every moment now. He whipped out his phone and took a few photos, knowing his mother would never believe what had just happened without photographic evidence. He was having enough trouble believing it himself. A baby girl. *His* baby girl.

'Would you like to cut the cord?' the midwife asked.

'I… Yes,' Jack found himself saying in a trance-like daze. He put his phone down and he did as the midwife instructed and watched as she put a clamp on the cord next to the baby's little tummy.

Harper was sobbing with relief and joy as she cradled the tiny baby against her breasts. 'Oh, Jack, isn't she beautiful?' The note of wonder in her tone sent another wave of emotion through him. Call him biased, but surely not *all* babies were as beautiful as his little baby?

'She is indeed.' He stroked a soft finger over the baby's downy head. 'She's so tiny. Like a doll.'

Harper gave him a speaking glance. 'She didn't feel too tiny a few minutes ago.'

Jack leaned down to press a kiss to Harper's forehead. 'You were amazing. So brave. I'm in awe of what you just did.'

Harper looked up at him with shining eyes. 'Thanks for being here. I would've hated to be alone.' She looked down at the baby again, her voice softening to a soothing coo as she said, 'Hey, little one. Sorry we haven't got a name for you yet.' The baby began nuzzling against Harper's chest, her tiny, mewling cries making Jack's heart squeeze as if it were in a vice.

'You can offer her the breast,' Meg said. 'Were you planning on breastfeeding?'

'I guess so…' Harper said. 'It's best for the baby, isn't it?'

'We like to encourage mums to try and breast-feed, but if it's too hard, don't beat yourself up about using formula,' the midwife assured her.

Harper helped the baby latch onto her breast and Jack wondered if he'd ever seen such a beau-tiful sight. A mother and her newborn baby. *His* baby. His little daughter. It was like a miracle to see her perfectly formed, tiny body. The little star-fish hands, her feet smaller than the length of his thumb, her downy head covered in jet-black hair, the same as his. He blinked and blinked again, fully expecting he would find himself back at his hotel penthouse, waking up from a weird dream. But no, he was in the delivery suite, watching his newborn daughter having her first feed. Emotions he had never felt before flooded through his body. Emotions he had resisted feeling for most of his adult life. Emotions that tugged on his chest as if strings were attached to his heart, pulling at the shield of armour he had built around it.

He was a father.

A dad.

His little girl needed him in her life. He had responsibilities now that were so important they surpassed everything he had achieved in his career so far. He would not—could not—allow anyone else to rear his child. It was his responsibility to see she had everything she needed to thrive. He had heard someone say that every childhood lasted a lifetime and it had resonated a little too well with him. There were aspects of his childhood he would do anything to prevent happening to his daughter.

The midwife finished cleaning up, and once the baby had finished feeding, she wrapped her in a soft blanket, and left them to continue to bond with her. Jack took some more photos with his phone, still finding it surreal to be a father. Had his own father felt this sense of awe and wonder at his birth? Jack had a handful of good memories of his father as a younger man but the slow and painful progression of his father's Parkinson's Disease had tainted many others. Jack had been sent to boarding school to spare him the worst of it. And he had been sent away for holiday camps as well because his father refused to travel. Home had ceased to be a home and was more of a hospice. A place of gloom and doom and disappointment. His father's death when Jack was eighteen had not devastated him, as it had his mother. His emotional response had been relief instead of grief. But now he was a father himself, he couldn't imagine wanting anything but the best for his daughter. He wanted to be fully present in raising her. He wanted to be there for her for as long as he lived. She would be seen and she would be heard.

The baby soon fell asleep and Harper glanced up at Jack again. 'Would you like to hold her?'

Jack couldn't remember ever holding a baby before, certainly not one so young. What if he didn't hold her correctly? Wasn't there something about their necks being fragile and needing proper support? What if the baby began to cry? What if she didn't recognise him as her father? 'I don't want to wake her. She looks so peaceful.'

Disappointment flickered briefly over Harper's face but then she covered it with bitterness. 'Would you prefer to have a paternity test done first?' Her tone was sharp as a scalpel, her grey-green eyes hard.

Jack had not even thought of asking for a paternity test. He knew most men in his position would do so and would be completely justified in asking for one, except he didn't for a moment doubt the baby was his. He couldn't explain why, it wasn't rational at all, just a feeling. And he wasn't normally the type of man to rely on feelings. But… that screwed-up little face topped with its liberal dusting of black hair did resemble him as a baby. And he felt connected to her in a way he couldn't explain. A connection that was almost spiritual. 'Is there any reason I should have one done?' he asked.

She shrugged one shoulder. 'I just thought you'd want one. I might have had numerous partners since you.'

'Have you?'

'No.' Her shoulders went down on a little sigh and she traced a gentle finger across the baby's tiny forehead.

Her confession surprised him and secretly delighted him. He had been celibate for the whole time too, but what were her reasons for not dating anyone since? 'Why?'

Another shrug, her gaze shifting from his. 'I'm not going to feed your already overblown ego by telling you I didn't fancy sleeping with anyone else after that night of…of amazing sex.' Her cheeks flushed a delicate shade of pink and she sank her teeth into her lower lip as if she wished she hadn't revealed quite so much.

Jack gave a lazy smile. 'Then I won't feed your ego either and tell you the same.'

Harper's gaze flicked back to his, her eyes as wide as dishes. Satellite dishes. 'Are you serious? You haven't slept with anyone since?' Her incredulous tone made him wonder if his reputation as a playboy had been a tad over-exaggerated. Sure, he didn't stay in a fling long, but he often had breaks between lovers. Long breaks. Not as long as nine months, but still. When he was working on a new hotel development he liked to focus. He put his private life on hold in the early stages of a project so he could concentrate his whole attention on the job at hand. And it paid off. He had brokered numerous deals and invested millions in spectacular hotel developments, which had built the Livingstone Hotel chain to a luxury brand that rivalled some of his biggest competitors. 'I've been busy securing a deal in Yorkshire.'

Another glimmer of bitterness shone in her eyes. 'Yes, I heard about that. You bought Rothwell Park.' Her resentful tone seemed to suggest she thought he had bought it deliberately to spite her.

'You know it?'

'My business partner, Ruby Pennington, grew up there with her grandmother. I visited once when I was about twelve. We had a wedding there recently—I did the photos. You probably saw it in the press or heard about it from Lucas Rothwell. Delphine Rainbird, the American actress.' She straightened her shoulders and added, 'Was it a coincidence or did you know I had a connection to the place?'

It was Jack's turn to shrug. 'Mere coincidence.'

The baby gave a tiny yawn and turned her head in Jack's direction, her dark eyes gazing at him like a baby owl.

'I think she wants you to hold her,' Harper said. 'She's starting to recognise your voice.'

Jack came closer and gently took the baby from Harper. He couldn't stop staring at her tiny features—the button nose, the rosebud mouth, the squinty little eyes that opened again as soon as he touched her and stared up at him without blinking, as if she didn't dare let him out of her sight. 'Hey, little one…' His voice caught on something rough at the back of his throat and he had to swallow to clear it. 'You've created quite a stir, young lady, turning up unannounced. You'll have to forgive us for being a little unprepared.'

Thing was, Jack was *never* unprepared. He was a planner, a box ticker, a details man who left nothing to chance. He never allowed himself to be surprised by anything. Meticulous planning removed the surprise element—mostly. But nothing was more surprising than to suddenly find himself the father of a baby girl.

She opened her little mouth and yawned again, and something in his chest flipped open like a faulty latch on a locked door. He was ambushed by unfamiliar feelings. Emotions he had never allowed free rein before. Emotions that had the potential to tilt his neat and controlled world on its axis. He fought those emotions, pushed and shoved them back where he could look at them from a safe distance, knowing they were there but still under his control. He could provide for his child and provide well. And he would provide for and support Harper too.

'Jack?' Harper's voice was tentative. 'I know you must think I'm an idiot for not knowing I was pregnant. If I had known, I would've told you straight away.'

'Why didn't you want to see me again?'

She chewed at one side of her mouth. 'I was ashamed of how I let you distract me from my work at the Tenterbury wedding. It was so unprofessional of me to be sneaking off upstairs with the best man. I have never done anything like that before or since. I'd made a pact with myself to never mix business with pleasure and you made me break it.'

'I seem to recall there was quite a lot of pleasure that night.' Jack still got shivers thinking about it. The fiery heat of attraction, the flirty banter that went on for hours until they dashed upstairs and engaged in the most mind-blowing sex of his life. Truth be told, he had avoided hooking up with anyone since because he wanted to linger over the memory of that night. To relive the tingling sensations, to revisit the incredible kisses and caresses that had stirred him so deeply.

And that episode of passionate lovemaking had produced this tiny infant—his daughter.

Harper's gaze avoided his and stared at the baby in his arms as if she too couldn't quite get her head around the fact they had made a baby. A worried look came over her face and she glanced up at him again. 'Parents usually have months and months to prepare for this. I didn't address a single word to her while I was carrying her. What if that damages her in some way? I didn't even eat properly most of the time.' She blew out a whoosh of air and added, 'But thankfully, I'm teetotal and a non-smoker.'

Jack looked down at the tiny bundle in his arms. 'She looks perfect in every way, so don't worry too much.' The baby opened her tiny mouth and gave a yawn and then opened her dark blue eyes and stared at him again. The tugging sensation in his chest was stronger this time and he took a deep breath to settle it. He took one of the baby's miniscule hands and marvelled at the tiny fingernails on the ends of fingers so small it didn't seem possible there was room for bones and ligaments and tendons inside. 'Hey, little one. What are we going to call you, hmm?'

'I don't want any way-out names,' Harper said. 'She'll be an adult a lot longer than she'll be a baby, so it should be a name that won't embarrass her as she gets older. But I don't want it to be too old-fashioned either.'

'I agree,' Jack said. 'Do you want to name her after someone? Your mother? Your grandmother?'

The flash of horror that flicked across Harper's face made him realise he hardly knew anything about her. But then, what did she know about him other than what she might have read in the gossip pages or online?

'No, there aren't any family names I'd want to inflict on my child.'

'Okay. My mother's name is Elizabeth, although she gets called Liz most of the time. Susannah is her middle name.'

Harper shifted her mouth from side to side. 'I like both but more as middle names.' She glanced at the baby thoughtfully and added, 'We could give her two middle names, I guess.'

'Why not? I have three.'

Harper turned to look at him again. 'Really? Isn't that a bit excessive?'

'A little, but apparently there were a lot of people to please when I was born,' Jack said.

'So what is your full name?'

'Jackson Sebastien Miles Rochester Livingstone.'

Her eyebrows lifted. 'Rochester? Seriously?'

Jack grinned. 'As in *Jane Eyre*? Yep, it was my paternal grandmother's maiden name.'

Harper looked back at the baby. 'What about Marli with an I? It's not too out there and it's not old-fashioned.'

Jack nodded. 'I like it too.' He looked down at the baby, who was now clutching one of his fingers in her tiny hand. A warm feeling spread through his chest and he smiled. 'Hello, Marli Elizabeth Susannah Livingstone.'

'Swan.' Harper's tone was adamant, her gaze as hard as stone.

'You do realise what the acronym of her name will be if you don't marry me? MESS.' It was a heck of a tactic to convince Harper to marry him, but he was prepared to use whatever was at his disposal.

Harper held her arms out for Marli, her expression faltering as if she could see the sense in his point but was too proud to admit it right there and then. 'I want to hold her now.'

Jack passed the baby back to her, his arms feeling strangely empty without the tiny bundle cradled there. He straightened and stood next to the bed. 'She belongs to both of us, Harper, so she should have both our names. We can hyphenate them after we get married.'

Her chin came up at a defiant height. 'I am not marrying you.'

'I probably need to work on my proposal but I want Marli to live with me. I don't want to be a part-time parent.'

'But you travel all over the world for your work.'

'You do too.'

'Not as much as you.' She looked back down at Marli and frowned. 'Although I have to go to Paris in six weeks.'

'For a wedding?'

'No, for a photo shoot for a book I've been asked to contribute to.' She stroked a gentle finger across the baby's forehead again, the action one of wonder, as if she couldn't quite believe she was holding a live baby. Her baby. His baby. *Their* baby. 'I have no idea how I'm going to be able to juggle work and the Paris trip now I've got a baby…' Her teeth began to savage her lip again and her small, neat chin began to tremble.

Jack placed his hand on the top of her right shoulder. 'We'll figure out how to do it together. She's both our responsibility and I am not going to let you do this alone, okay?'

She flicked him an upwards glance. 'I can only imagine what the press is going to make of this. We're practically strangers and now we've got a baby.'

'It doesn't mean we can't be great parents or a well-functioning couple,' Jack said, and, reaching into his trouser pocket, took out Harper's earring. 'By the way, I have something of yours you left behind last time we met.'

Harper looked at the earring for a brief moment, then took it from his open palm and put it next to her phone and purse on the table next to the hospital bed. 'Yes, well, I have something of yours too.' She passed the baby back to him with a wry twist of her mouth. 'Your baby.'

CHAPTER THREE

JACK SAT ON the chair beside the bed holding Marli while Harper had a shower. The nurse had brought in a portable crib for the baby but he hadn't yet transferred her to it. He didn't want to risk waking her—especially while her mother was out of the room. But neither did he want to miss out on these precious early moments of her life. He balanced Marli in one arm and took out his phone and called his mother. 'Are you sitting down?' he said when she answered.

'Oh, darling, don't tell me you're finally madly in love?' The excitement in his mother's tone was unmistakable. And annoying because he had no intention of ever falling in love.

'No, but I am going to get married.'

'You can't possibly marry someone you don't love.'

'I can because she's the mother of my baby,' Jack said.

The silence was short but intense, like the ticking of a time bomb. *Tick. Tick. Tick…*

'Your…*what*?' His mother's voice was a screech of shock.

'I have a baby daughter just a few minutes old.'

'Oh, my God, but why didn't you tell me before now? I didn't even know you were dating anyone long-term. When can I see the baby? What did you call her? Oh, I'm so excited I can barely stand it. I have to go shopping and get her a present. Lots of presents and toys and dolls and a proper teddy bear. Oh, I can't believe I'm finally a granny. But you haven't even told me your fiancée's name. Do I know her? Have I met her?' The questions were like bullets fired out of an automatic weapon. 'When can I see the baby? Can I come now? Where are you? In London? Oh, I can't wait to hold her. I never thought this day would come. I think I'm going to faint with shock.'

'Mum, calm down.'

'Don't tell me to calm down on the most exciting day of my life since I had you,' his mother said. 'If I wasn't so excited, I'd be furious with you for not telling me you were expecting a child. How could you have robbed me of the joy of anticipating becoming a grandmother? Did you do it deliberately? I never thought you could be so mean.'

'I only found out half an hour before she was born.'

'What?'

'My…fiancée—' Jack decided to refer to Harper as his bride-to-be because he was not going to take no for an answer '—had what's called a cryptic pregnancy. She only found out herself just before she delivered.'

'Oh, my goodness! I've heard about that sort of thing but I never believed it was possible. How could she not know? You nearly kicked your way out of my abdomen when I carried you. And my stomach still has the stretch marks to prove it.' His mother paused to draw breath and then continued, 'But surely you would have noticed the changes in her body, especially if you were…you know… intimate with her all this time.'

'I wasn't with her over the last nine months,' Jack said, already hating how this was going to sound to his conservative mother, married for years to one man. 'We had a one-night stand and—'

'Oh, Jack, is this young woman a gold-digger? I mean, this is an old trick but a good one. You're a handsome billionaire. Who wouldn't want to trap you into a shotgun marriage?'

Jack pinched the bridge of his nose and hoped his daughter was too young to understand the words her grandmother was saying about her mother. 'Mum, I want to marry Harper. No one's forcing me to do anything. In fact, I have to convince her to agree to it. She's not exactly been too keen so far on the idea.'

'What? But you're a prize catch!'

'I don't think Harper quite sees me that way.'

The bathroom door opened and Harper came out in a fresh hospital gown and her hair wrapped turban-like in a towel.

'That's another trick—playing hard to get.' His mother's voice was loud enough to wake the dead in the morgue downstairs. 'Have you asked for a paternity test? You must insist on one, Jack. Don't get too attached to the baby until you're sure it's yours. And for God's sake, don't marry that girl unless you're absolutely sure she's being straight with you.'

Jack clenched his jaw and gave Harper an apologetic glance. 'Mum, I have to go. I'll arrange a time for you to meet Marli Elizabeth Susannah in the next day or two.'

'You named her after me?' His mother's tone softened. 'Oh, how sweet of you.'

'It was Harper's idea, actually.'

Another short, tight silence.

'Well, I'll look forward to meeting her too,' his

mother said. 'Send me some photos? I won't be-lieve I'm a grandmother until I see proof.'

'Sending them now. Bye.' Jack ended the call and deftly sent some photos of the baby to his mother. 'Sorry you had to hear that.' He put his phone back down and looked at Harper, who was now sitting on the bed with a pinched look on her face.

'See? I told you. A paternity test is necessary.'

'And I told you I don't need one,' Jack said.

Harper bounced off the bed and then winced as if she'd forgotten she had given birth less than an hour ago. 'I'm going to have one done no matter what you say. I don't want people speculating or calling me a flipping gold-digger.' She came over and took the baby from him to cradle her close and protectively against her chest. 'That's why mar-riage is out of the question. Who's ever going to believe we're in love?'

'What's love got to do with anything? We can have a perfectly satisfying relationship without being in love with each other. That one night to-gether nine months ago proved that.'

Harper's mouth dropped open. 'What? You don't believe in love in marriage? Is that what you're truly saying?'

'I'm saying it's not as necessary as you might

think,' Jack said. 'Obviously it's the ideal, but plenty of relationships survive on much less than that.'

'Survive, yes, but do they thrive?' Harper placed the baby gently in the crib and covered her with the pink blanket, tucking in the edges tenderly. 'I want the best environment for Marli. I want her surrounded by love. I don't want her to be around people who can't bear the sight of each other.'

Jack came over to stand behind her, placing his hands on her shoulders. 'What's this talk of us not liking each other, hmm?'

She turned to face him, her expression guarded. 'We don't know each other, Jack.'

He trailed a lazy finger down the curve of her cheek. 'I know what turns you on.' He lowered his voice to a husky drawl. 'And you know what turns me on.' He sent his finger over the plump cushion of her lower lip. 'I couldn't get you out of my mind. It's why I wanted to see you again. I wanted to make sure I hadn't imagined how good it was between us.'

She cast him a wary look from beneath her lowered lashes. 'Did you really not hook up with anyone since me?'

Jack gently squeezed both her shoulders. 'Not a single person. Nine months is a bit of a record for me. But as I said, I was busy negotiating the deal on Rockwell Park and trying to convince you to see me again.'

'Because of my earring?'

'It looks like a valuable one.'

'Sentimental value, mostly. I bought those earrings with my first paycheck as a photographer.' She dipped out from under his light hold and gave a movement of her lips that wasn't anywhere near a smile and more of a grimace. 'Can I see the photos you took?'

'Sure.' Jack took out his phone but, rather than hand it to her, held it up so they could stand shoulder to shoulder to scroll through the shots. 'I can't say I'm as good a photographer as you, but our baby girl is pretty photogenic, wouldn't you say?'

'I can't believe I just had a baby...' Harper's voice cracked over the words. 'And what sort of photographer am I if I haven't taken a single shot of her? My phone is flat and my camera is at the office.'

Jack handed her his phone. 'Use mine.'

She took the phone from him and moved closer to the crib. She aimed the lens at various angles, taking snap after snap of Marli. She straightened and looked at him again. 'What if I take some of you with her?'

'Good idea,' Jack said. He carefully scooped Marli out of the crib and congratulated himself on not disturbing her sleep. In spite of his lack of preparation, maybe he wouldn't do such a bad job of being a father after all.

'Stand over there where the light is better,' Harper said. 'Now look down at her as if she is the most wonderful thing you've ever seen.'

'She is the most wonderful thing I've ever seen.' Jack held his baby girl against his chest, amazed at how peaceful she looked. 'Looks as if she's got your nose and mouth.'

'You think?'

'Definitely.'

Harper stopped snapping photos to come over to stand next to him to gaze down at the baby in his arms. She was so close he could smell the fruity fragrance of the shampoo she had used in the shower. He slipped an arm around her waist in order to draw her closer, but she jerked back from him as if his touch burnt her.

Her grey-green eyes glittered like those of a cornered cat. 'I know what you're doing.'

'What am I doing?'

She folded her arms across her middle in a keep-away-from-me gesture. 'You're trying to charm me into marrying you, but it won't work. I know it's a hackneyed phrase, but you're the last man on earth I would ever consider marrying. The point is, I don't want to marry anyone.'

Jack raised one of his eyebrows. 'That's kind of ironic given your line of work—wedding photography.'

'Yes, well, I like photographing weddings but it doesn't mean I want the fairy tale for myself.'

'See? We're perfectly suited for each other. We're both cynical about love.'

'I didn't say I was cynical about love.'

'Marriage, then?"

'I accept some marriages last years. Whether both parties are happy or not is another question.'

'What about your parents? Were they happily married?'

'No.'

'How long were they together?'

Harper turned away to straighten the bed linen as if she were the nurse on duty instead of a new mother who should be resting. 'Long enough for my father to get my mother pregnant.' She turned and faced him with a stony expression. 'When he found out she was carrying me and she refused to have an abortion, he dumped her and went back to his wife and family. The wife and family he had told her for months he was going to leave for her, but it was a pack of lies.'

'That must've been tough on your mother.'

'It was.'

'And tough on you too, once you were old enough to understand.'

'Yes, knowing your biological father wanted to get rid of you before you were born doesn't exactly build one's self-esteem.' The bitterness in her tone was raw, shadows of deep hurt in her eyes.

'Shouldn't you call your mother to tell her about the baby?'

Harper gave a hollow laugh that wasn't quite a laugh and sat back on the edge of the bed. 'No can do. She's been dead since I was eight.'

Jack could only imagine how devastating such a loss could have been to a young child. 'I'm sorry to hear that. How did she die?'

'Suicide.' Harper expelled a ragged breath and added, 'I found her.'

'God, Harper, that's awful.' He came over to sit beside her on the hospital bed, taking one of her hands in his. 'So who brought you up? Did your father step in?'

She pulled her hand away and rose from the bed, her arms going around her body once more. It was as if she didn't want to be comforted or supported. Or maybe it was because no one had ever been there for her before. It explained a lot about her feisty nature and independent streak. She didn't allow people too close in case they let her down or deserted her.

'He was contacted by the authorities and he promised to come and get me from emergency foster care but he always cancelled at the last minute or had some paltry excuse for why I couldn't come and live with him. I spent years of my life languishing in foster care, moving from home to home, waiting for him, stupidly believing his empty promises until I finally realised I was on my own.'

'It sounds like you were better off without him,' Jack said. He looked at his sleeping daughter and wondered how any man could walk away from his own flesh and blood. While he might not have planned to be a father, there was no way he could ever turn his back on his own child. He would always be there for her, to provide and protect and encourage her to thrive and reach her potential. And he figured the best way to do it was to marry Harper so they could be a family. Clearly she had not had a happy and fulfilling childhood—all the more reason for him to step in and help her raise their child. 'I can't imagine how disappointing that must have been for you. Do you have any other relatives? Aunts, uncles? Grandparents?'

'No one wanted me.' Her tone was devoid of emotion and yet he sensed an undercurrent of lingering pain and disillusionment.

Jack watched her hover over Marli's crib, her

fierce expression reminding him of a mother lion protecting her cub. She stroked her hand over the baby's head and Marli made a soft sound as if she recognised her mother's gentle touch. 'I know my mother loved me in her way. But she struggled badly with her mental health. She drank to self-medicate and misused prescription drugs. It's why I don't drink alcohol and I rarely take anything, not even paracetamol.'

'I'm in awe of your pain threshold, both physical and emotional,' Jack said, coming to stand next to her by the crib.

There was a silence broken only by the baby's soft snuffling sounds.

'Jack?' Harper's voice was quiet and tentative, her gaze still focused on the baby. 'Promise me you won't abandon her? Please? No matter what our relationship is, don't ever abandon Marli.'

Jack placed his hands on her hips and gently turned her to face him. Her features were cast in lines of worry. He brushed a slow-moving finger down the curve of her cheek, his eyes holding hers. 'I will never abandon her. I'll do everything in my power to give her a happy and fulfilling life.'

Her gaze lowered to his mouth and the tip of her tongue came out and swept over her own lips. 'Thank you.'

Jack bent down and placed his mouth on hers

in a barely touching kiss. A soft press down that should have ended there but somehow didn't. Harper moved closer, his arms tightened around her and his mouth came down again to hers, moving against hers in a kiss that was gentle and yet throbbed with banked-down passion. He could feel it pulsing in his body in response to her taste and touch. The sweet taste and sensual touch he had craved and dreamed of for the last nine months. Her mouth was an exotic fruit and he wanted to feast on its sweetness until he was drunk from it. She responded to his kiss with a breathless sound that sent a shiver down his spine, her arms snaking around his neck to link behind his head.

But then Harper suddenly pulled back from his embrace and rapid-blinked, as if shocked at what had just occurred. 'I'm sorry. I didn't mean that to happen.' She raised a flustered hand to her face and pushed back her still damp hair. 'It must be hormones or something.' Her cheeks were bright pink, her gaze quickly averted.

'Don't apologise.'

She moved to the other side of the bed as if she wanted a boundary line to stand behind. 'I don't want you to get the wrong idea…to lead you on or anything.'

Jack ran a hand through his hair, trying to get his own hormones to settle down. 'It's been a pretty crazy couple of hours. You probably need to get some sleep.'

'Yes… I am a little tired…'

That would have to be the biggest understatement he had ever heard. Her eyes had dark circles beneath them, her face was drawn and her shoulders were drooping with fatigue. He wanted to hug her, to hold her, to reassure her, but her expression and posture warned him to keep his distance. 'Is there anything I can get you before I go? A drink? Food?'

She chewed one side of her mouth and glanced at the baby, a frown pulling at her brow. 'I have nothing for her. No clothes to take her home in. No baby equipment or—'

'I'll take care of it first thing tomorrow,' Jack said with far more confidence than he felt. He knew zilch about what babies needed but surely his mother or a shop assistant would help.

'I didn't come in my car to the hospital. I caught a cab, so you'll need to get a baby seat for your car.'

'Right…' Jack wasn't sure a baby seat would even fit in his top-model sports car.

'You don't happen to have a phone charger on you, do you? I need to call my friends.'

'I'll get you one from one of the doctors or nurses.'

'Thank you.'

Jack found a phone charger within a few minutes and came back to find Harper curled up on the bed, facing the crib but fast asleep. He plugged in her phone and left it on the bedside table. He stood looking down at her for a long moment, still trying to come to terms with what had happened in the last couple of hours. He had had some pretty eventful days in his life but this one surely topped the lot.

CHAPTER FOUR

'YOU'VE HAD A *WHAT*?' Ruby and Aerin gasped in unison when Harper called them later that night on a video call.

'It wasn't backache, I mean, I did have backache, but it was actually labour,' Harper explained about her cryptic pregnancy, still finding it hard to believe herself. And she wouldn't have believed it if her baby wasn't lying in the crib next to her bed, fast asleep after her last feed.

'But you didn't even *look* pregnant,' Ruby said in a stunned tone.

'You did have a certain glow about you, though,' Aerin put in. 'And you were eating for two. Remember that night when you cleared the platter Ruby prepared? You seemed unusually hungry, especially since you're nearly always dieting.'

Harper didn't have a slim build like her business partners. She had struggled with accepting her more statuesque form for years. But now she had produced a baby, she had a new respect for her body. She was amazed at what her body had done in nurturing and growing a baby and then delivering it. She angled the camera so the girls could see Marli. 'Here's my baby girl. What do you think of her?'

'Oh, she's just divine,' Aerin said with wondrous awe in her voice.

'What a sweet little face,' Ruby said with equal adoration. 'She's like a doll.'

'That's what her father said.'

'Who *is* her father?' Ruby asked. 'Or can I take a wild guess and say it's Jack Livingstone?'

'Was he there for the birth?' Aerin chipped in.

Harper took a breath and released it in a not quite steady stream. 'Jack is Marli's father. And yes, he managed to get here in time for the birth.' Another point in his favour. He had mopped her brow, held her hand and had his practically crushed in return, but had he flinched? Had he complained? Had he walked away and denied parenthood?

No.

He was all in.

And insisting on marrying her, no less.

Harper's mother had birthed her all alone, all the while knowing her baby's father hadn't wanted to meet his child. Hadn't wanted anything to do with his baby girl or her mother. Now that she had given birth herself, Harper realised how awfully lonely and terrifying it must have been for her poor mother.

'Was he…surprised? Shocked?' Aerin asked.

'Probably about the same as me,' Harper said. 'I'm glad he was here, though. With you two out of town, I didn't know who else to call.' It wasn't as if she had a mother of her own to call. Jack had turned up at her request and got there in time to see his baby come into the world. Harper recalled the way he had supported her and his gentle handling of their daughter and fought against the feelings the vision stirred in her chest.

But she was not in love with her baby's father. Jack Livingstone was practically a stranger. He might be devilishly attractive and utterly charming, but she was *not* going to fall in love with him.

And hot damn, she would not think about *that* kiss.

'So, how's it going to go with you two bringing up a baby?' Ruby asked. 'I take it he wants to be involved?'

'He wants to marry me.'

'Marry you?' Aerin gasped again in shock. 'What did you say?'

'No, of course,' Harper said. 'Why would I marry him just because he's the father of my baby?'

'What if he's in love with you?' Ruby said.

'I mean, he wanted to see you again but you always refused.'

Harper gave a clipped laugh of cynicism. 'Jack isn't used to women saying no to him. I was a challenge he couldn't resist.'

'At least he offered to support you,' Aerin said. 'That's definitely a point in his favour.'

Harper could think of dozens of points in his favour—his strong and capable take-charge attitude, his work ethic, his unflappable temperament, his drive for success. And then there was his tall and athletic build, his too-handsome features, the blue eyes that were as dark as a mountain tarn, his lean and chiselled jaw, his swept-back jet-black hair, his long, straight nose and his sensually carved mouth…

Argh. She must *not* think about his mouth and how it felt against her lips. Sensual and seductive, soft and yet commanding. A mouth that could distract her from all of her carefully constructed goals. A mouth that could beguile and bewitch and befuddle her until she couldn't control herself.

But doubts about Jack supporting his child for the long haul circled around her head. Babies were cute, but toddlers could be a handful. And what about the rollercoaster time of puberty and adolescence? What if the novelty of being a father wore off sooner rather than later? What if he abandoned

Marli the way Harper had been abandoned by her own father? She couldn't allow that to happen to her little girl. The marriage Jack was proposing seemed a clinical sort of arrangement. What exactly would it entail? And how could she agree to spend her life with a man who openly admitted to not loving her? Or even believing in love? He said he had been celibate for the last nine months but she couldn't see him being celibate for the duration of their marriage. Or would he expect they would sleep together, raise their child together but not fall in love? She had slept with him once and her heart had almost been his. Almost. Sleeping with him again would be asking for the sort of trouble she had spent her life avoiding.

Love trouble.

Deep trouble.

Inescapable trouble.

Marli woke and gave a mewling cry, her little arms waving about her head.

'I'd better see to her,' Harper said. 'Come and meet her as soon as you get back to London.'

'I'll organise a baby shower for you,' Aerin said. 'I know it's meant to be before the birth, but under these circumstances, what does it matter?'

'That would be nice,' Harper said. 'I have nothing for her, although Jack promised to get me some stuff before we take her home tomorrow.' But where would home be? His place or hers?

'We'll do everything we can to help you, Harper,' Ruby said. 'It'll be a juggle with the bookings we've got coming up but you can take maternity leave if you want. We can get a stand-in photographer for a few weeks. You'll need time to bond with Marli.'

'But I still have to go to Paris in six weeks,' Harper said. 'No one can go in my place. It's my work they want to feature. It's a dream come true for me and I can't back out at the last minute.'

'Then concentrate on that and leave the weddings to us,' Ruby said. 'And give that gorgeous little munchkin a cuddle from me. Tell her Aunty Ruby already loves her to bits and her Uncle Lucas will be besotted as soon as he sees her.'

Harper smiled in spite of her worries for the future. Ruby was like a sister to her and so was Aerin. Through thick and thin, flood and drought and confidence and doubt, they stood by her and she stood by them. What did she need a husband for?

Especially one as dangerously distracting as Jack Livingstone.

Jack had never been in a baby goods store in his life. He stood surrounded by pastel colours, soft, fluffy toys, numerous clothes in a variety of sizes, cots and prams and pushers and baby carriers and bassinets and car seats and change tables and nappies and sippy cups and bottles and even breast pump machines. How could one tiny infant need all this stuff? Where was he supposed to start? He picked up a pink and white unicorn with a gold horn on its head and inadvertently pressed the start button on its stomach and a soothing lullaby started to play. The song from his own childhood stirred deeply buried memories of being surrounded by parents and two sets of grandparents who loved and nurtured him. Relatives who one by one had disappeared through death and disease, leaving only his mother and him still standing.

Love came with a price—loss.

Terrible, heartbreaking, unavoidable loss.

His mother had lost his father by degrees, the man she adored becoming frail and more and more difficult as the ravages of his Parkinson's set in. And Jack had lost his father too, watching as his strong and capable body and sharp mind deteriorated, leaving him the shell of a man who had fought every inch of the way to hide his vulnerability.

And because of his father's determination to conceal his increasing disability, the family hotel business had been all but destroyed by his father's mismanagement, leaving Jack to pick up the pieces to rebuild the Livingstone Hotel brand to make it even better than before. But not before watching as precious heirloom after precious heirloom and property after property were sold to meet the eye-watering debts. Losses that to this day he hated thinking about. Which was why he was always on the hunt for a new property to develop, to make up for those he had lost.

Jack figured the only way to avoid such devastating losses in his own life was not to love in the first place. To keep his emotions in check. In control. Under lock and key.

Safe.

A middle-aged woman came over with a smile on her face. 'May I help you with anything?'

Jack put the unicorn down, packing his memories away like old clothes that were no longer his size. 'My fiancée and I have just had a baby girl and I need to get some gear.' Call him stubborn but he was determined to keep calling Harper his fiancée.

The woman's eyes lit up. 'Congratulations. What things did you have in mind?'

Jack picked up a pink onesie that looked about the right size for Marli. 'Let's start with this and go from there.'

* * *

Harper was putting Marli back in her crib after a feed the next morning, when Jack came in carrying bulging bags from a well-known brand of babywear. 'Looks like you've been busy.'

'Just a little.' Jack put the bags on the bed and came over to gaze down at the baby. 'How did she sleep?'

'Like a baby.'

He flashed a grin at her that shot an arrow straight to her heart. She had to be careful not to fall for his disarming charm. She had to keep her emotions out of their relationship…whatever their relationship was now. They were parents of a tiny baby. They were former lovers but, since it had only been a one-night stand, did that even count as a fling? It was a passing moment in time that had brought about the birth of their child.

'You want to have a look at the things I got? The rest is back at my hotel.'

Harper leaned on her hands and pulled her shoulders back. 'Is that where you live? In one of your hotels?'

He gave a loose shrug of one impossibly broad shoulder. 'It makes sense to base myself in the flagship hotel in London so I can keep an eye on things.'

Harper pushed herself off the bed and moved

around the other side, folding her arms across the middle of her body. 'I hope you're not expecting our child to live in a hotel?' She had lived in temporary accommodation throughout her childhood—bedsits, caravan parks, shelters and then foster care. None of which were permanent homes. None of which felt like *her* home.

'I expect my child to live with me and her mother.' There was a chord of determination in his tone. 'How can I be a fully present and involved father if I only see Marli every second weekend?'

Harper sent him a look that was so frosty it could have frozen the water in the jug on her tray table. 'I told you I'm not marrying you.'

'Where do you live?'

'I live in a flat in South Kensington.' 'Flat' was too generous a term for the tiny one-bedroom place she paid an exorbitant rent for and Harper wondered how long it would take him to realise it.

'How many bedrooms?'

Mmm…not long, apparently. She couldn't hold his steely gaze and blew out her breath on a sigh. 'One.'

'Hardly big enough to raise a family.' His voice was just shy of condescending.

Harper raised her gaze back to his. 'It will be fine for now, and besides, it's just Marli and me. I can move to a bigger place when she's a bit older.' *When I've had time to adjust to becoming a mother*, she could have added but didn't. But would she *ever* adjust? She was still reeling from the shock of finding herself the mother of a baby. She had spent the night staring at her tiny daughter, chastising herself for not having recognised she was pregnant. Torturing herself with all the what-ifs…what if she had been a drinker? What if she had been a six-coffees-a-day person? What if she had been the sort of person to pop pills whenever she got the teeniest ache or pain? What if she had eaten some of those listeria-contaminated foods you weren't supposed to eat while pregnant? She could have inadvertently harmed her baby, causing her child irreparable damage, ruining Marli's potential all because she had not for a moment suspected she was pregnant.

'I'll buy a house for us to live in,' Jack said. 'Problem solved.'

Harper gave a startled laugh. 'Nice to be able to just go and buy oneself a house, especially in London, where the price of real estate is out of most people's reach.'

'I'm not most people. I own a chain of luxury hotels and can afford to buy my child and my fiancée a nice home.'

'Which you seem to think I'll meekly agree to live in with you.'

Jack gave her a sardonic look. 'There's not too much about you that's meek but I'm hoping you'll see the practical advantages of our living with each other.'

Harper upped her chin, shooting him a blistering glare. 'Practicalities meaning you expect me to dive head first into your bed?'

His dark blue eyes glinted as if he was thinking about how she'd done exactly that nine months ago. Trouble was, once she'd got into his bed that night, she hadn't wanted to get out. And that was something she wasn't prepared to risk happening again. He was too attractive, too addictive, too everything. She had no willpower around him. He only had to look at her a certain way and her body would betray her. No one had ever made love to her the way Jack Livingstone had. He had made her pleasure a priority. He had made her feel things she had never felt before. He had touched every inch of her body and celebrated it, worshipped and revered it as if it was the most beautiful and sexy body he had ever encountered. She might have given birth only the day before, but even *thinking* about what he had made her feel on that night nine months ago gave her shivers all over again.

'Isn't that part of the marriage deal?' he asked. 'The couple agree to worship each other's bodies for the rest of their lives?'

Harper snorted. 'As if you would agree to be faithful to one person for the rest of your life. You're a playboy, for pity's sake.'

His expression became grave. 'You have my word, Harper. I will remain faithful but I insist it be a real marriage. And it goes without saying, I expect you to be faithful to me.'

The baby made a sound and Harper went to her crib to check on her. But Jack had moved too, and they stood side by side, looking down at their daughter, who had settled back to sleep with a soft little sigh. Harper was conscious of how his shirt sleeve was brushing the bare skin of her arm. Conscious of the citrus and spice of his aftershave that teased her senses like a stupefying elixir. Conscious of his every breath and the hectic racing of her own pulse.

Jack suddenly turned to look at her and her heart slipped like a stiletto on black ice. His arresting blue eyes had been the first thing she had noticed about him nine months ago. Breath-snatching eyes, fringed with enviably long and thick ink-black lashes, his eyebrows twin dark slashes above an intelligent brow. But there were twin smudges beneath his eyes, too, as if he hadn't slept well the night before. It made her realise with a jolt she hadn't talked to him about how he felt about becoming a father.

She had been too consumed by her own shock and surprise to take a moment to reflect on his reaction.

'Jack?' Her voice came out whisper-soft. 'Are you…happy to be a father?'

He gave a slow blink and then let out a serrated sigh. 'If anyone had asked me even a week ago if I'd be happy to be a father, I would have flatly said no. It isn't something I have ever aspired to being. But now Marli's here…' He glanced at their child sleeping in the crib and added in a tone rough around the edges, 'I'm happy, proud, gobsmacked and overwhelmed with the desire to protect her no matter what.'

Harper was well aware that she was one of the 'no matter what's. Her refusal to marry him was an obstacle he was determined to remove. But how could she marry him without love? She point blank refused to examine her feelings for him. She had buried them as soon as she had left his hotel room that night. What sort of sex-dazzled fool fell in love with a man after a one-night stand? She had confused fabulous sex with full-on love. The feel-good hormone oxytocin released after multiple orgasms had bewitched her into thinking he was The One and Only.

He wasn't.

He couldn't be.

She wouldn't *let* him be. That was why she had

got the hell out of his hotel room before it could happen. But he was the father of her baby. And, while Harper's feelings could be ignored and denied or filed away, their baby could not be so easily dismissed. Marli was a living, breathing entity—a little human they had created together.

'What about you?' Jack asked. 'Are you happy to be a mother?'

Harper nibbled at her lower lip for a moment. 'I guess I'm a bit like you. I didn't plan to be a parent. I didn't yearn for it like my friends do. I've always been career-focused.' Her shoulders slumped on another sigh. 'What if I'm not a good mother? What if I mess up her life or something? It's not like I had the best role models for parents. My father didn't want me at all and my mother checked out when it all got too much for her. When *I* got too much for her.'

Jack's warm, strong hands came down on her shoulders, anchoring her. 'You blame yourself? You were only a child. It wasn't your fault she died the way she did.'

Harper lowered her gaze to the open neck of his shirt, where she could see the sprinkling of dark hair that covered his broad chest. 'It was my fault. I didn't get home from school at the usual time.' She released a ragged breath and continued, 'I found a stray kitten on my way home. I stopped to play with it. I lost track of time. I got home and…and, well, I found her on the sofa with an empty bottle of pills and an empty bottle of wine next to her. I called an ambulance but she couldn't be resuscitated.'

'Oh, Harper…' His arms wrapped around her and he brought her closer to his chest in a hug. 'You mustn't blame yourself. It sounds like your mother had some pretty complex issues that had nothing to do with you.'

'But they *were* to do with me,' Harper insisted, wishing it was otherwise, but in her heart, she knew she was to blame for everything. She pushed out of his embrace to look up at him through the glitter of sudden tears. 'If I hadn't been conceived, my mother might have realised in time the mistake it was to get involved with a married man. If I hadn't been born, my mother might have had the life of happiness and fulfilment she had envisaged as a romantic young girl. She might have found someone who would love her the way she deserved to be loved, someone who had wanted to raise a family and grow old with her. Someone who wouldn't lie and make promises he had no intention of keeping. But instead, she died a lonely death in a run-down flat at the wrong end of town. How is that not my fault?' She brushed at her eyes with an impatient hand, her chest tight with barely suppressed emotion. Emotion she normally controlled so well. Emotion she normally didn't allow herself to feel. 'Sorry. It's not like me to get so emotional.'

'Harper, you've just had a baby,' Jack said, taking her by the hands in a gentle but supportive hold. 'Your emotions, let alone your hormones, are all over the place.'

Harper looked into his concerned midnight-blue gaze and wondered if his emotions were in anything like the turmoil hers were. Like her, he had become a parent without warning, without preparation, without planning. 'We come from two different worlds, Jack. You come from a life of privilege. I've come from poverty. How can we possibly raise a child together?'

'We both love our little girl. That's the most important thing right now. Becoming a family for Marli's sake.'

It sounded so tempting. So very dangerously tempting. Her daughter would have everything Harper had not. Marli would not grow up wanting things she could not have, dreaming of adventures she would never get to experience. She would have everything money could buy. She would have two parents who loved her. Two parents who wanted the best for her.

But what would Harper have?

A husband who had only married her because he wanted to help raise his child. Not because he loved Harper for herself. A convenient marriage was not in her game plan. Any marriage, for that matter. Any relationship that would compromise her ability to make her creative mark on the world was out of the question.

Except…there was Marli to consider now…

Her daughter already had more love and commitment from her father in the first day of her life than Harper had ever received from hers in her whole lifetime. Although Marli's arrival had been a shock to Jack—as it had been to Harper—he hadn't shirked from his responsibilities. He hadn't even insisted on a paternity test. He had been all in from the moment he heard she was about to have his child. If Harper refused to marry him, it would certainly make it harder for him to be fully present in Marli's life. Did she want her little girl to have a part-time dad? Better than no dad at all, but still…

Harper slipped her hands out of his hold and gave him a wry look. 'You don't give up without a heck of a fight, do you?'

His flash of a grin did mortal damage to her determination to resist his outrageous proposal. 'When I want something, I do everything in my power to get it.'

And wasn't that the heart of Harper's problem in

a crinkly, uncrackable nutshell? Jack Livingstone had way more power than she did. Way, way more. And he was ruthless enough to use it.

CHAPTER FIVE

HARPER MOVED TO the bed where Jack had left the shopping bags. She began to take the items out and laid them out, but her forehead was creased in a frown as if none of what she was seeing pleased her.

'What? You don't like what I got?' Jack asked. 'The shop assistant helped me with the sizing. And Marli will grow into anything that's a bit big.'

Harper held up the little pink onesie, the first thing he had selected in the shop. 'You bought a lot of pink things.'

'Yes, well, isn't that what you dress baby girls in?'

She glanced at him over her shoulder, then turned back to pick up yet another pink outfit. 'Girls can wear other colours, even blue. It would look good with her skin tone and her eyes.' Which he was ridiculously proud to note were his skin tone and eye colour.

'But won't people think she's a boy?'

Harper turned to face him, her expression now unreadable except for a hard glitter in her eyes. 'Would you have preferred a boy?'

Jack whooshed out a breath, not sure where this was leading. 'It's not something I've ever thought about, to be honest. I never saw myself becoming a father. But to have a healthy child of either sex is surely something to be grateful for? And even if she wasn't healthy, I would still want to be there for her.'

Harper turned back and folded the velour outfit and placed it on the bed next to the pink beribboned teddy bear he'd bought. 'I think we should press pause on the marriage conversation until I get my head around being a mother. There's a lot to get used to…and with my hormones all over the place, I don't think this is a good time to make such a momentous decision.'

On one level, Jack could see the sense in what she was saying. Emotionally driven decisions were often the ones people regretted in the long run. That was why he never made them. Never got emotionally invested. He kept his emotions out of all business decisions, but he was determined to marry the mother of his child. He could not countenance any other option. 'Okay, we'll leave it for now. But I want your answer after we come back from Paris.'

Harper swung back to stare at him. 'You'll come with me?'

'But of course. How else will you look after Marli if I'm not there to help?' Jack had no clue how to look after a baby for hours on end, but he was on a crash course to learn. He wasn't sure how he was going to juggle his busy diary, but he had a good team of staff who would step up in his absence.

'I could engage a nanny... Lots of working women do.' Something about Harper's tone suggested it wasn't something she was completely convinced was the right choice for her. But then, there was so much she hadn't had time to think through about becoming a mother. Jack was conscious that the implications of parenthood, particularly in the early weeks and months, were likely to impact more on Harper than him, especially if she wanted to continue breastfeeding.

'You could but I would prefer to be as involved as I can, especially in these early months. They're meant to be important for proper emotional attachment.'

Harper's expression was cynical. 'I thought you didn't believe in emotional attachment?'

'Not in a romantic sense, but bringing up a child

is different. They need secure emotional attachment to their parents and caregivers.'

'Yes, well, I know that more than most.' Harper picked up the lullaby-playing unicorn and pressed the button on its tummy. The sweet strains of the lullaby filled the silence and her expression became wistful. 'I used to have a teddy bear that played this song but I lost it between foster homes.' She put the unicorn down and her expression became masked, as if revisiting that childhood memory had been more painful than she wanted to admit.

'It must have been hard moving from place to place.'

'I survived.'

But at what cost? There was a hard shell to her personality that reminded Jack of his own emotional armour. Was that why he had felt so drawn to her all those months ago? Seeing in Harper Swan a mirror image of himself? A person who knew what they wanted out of life and was determined to let no one and nothing get in their way. Who would let no one get close enough to hurt them. Who would let no one take advantage of them or disappoint them. Who was ruthlessly determined to keep themselves safe at all costs.

And right now he needed his own ruthless determination more than ever, for he was not going to rest until he had made Harper his bride.

Harper was discharged from hospital the following morning. She was privately impressed with how she had convinced the nursing staff at how well she was coping with sudden motherhood. But she had always been good at acting. Pretending she was fine when she was really struggling. Masking her true feelings so others didn't suspect she was feeling vulnerable and alone. Adopting a confident I've-got-this manner when she had no clue what she was doing.

Jack came at the agreed time to collect her and Marli. Harper had to push her feelings even further out of sight, squashing them so deep inside her chest she could feel them fluttering under her ribcage like a flock of frantic finches. What if she couldn't feed Marli properly? What if Marli lost weight and cried all night? What if she couldn't juggle work and caring for her child? A nanny was out of the question. It brought back too many memories of being looked after by strangers in foster care. People who came and went in her life, some of them caring, others not so much. How could she leave her child in the care of someone she didn't know or trust?

You trust Jack.

Did she, though? She hardly knew him, and yet there was something strong and dependable about Jack Livingstone. Something that had drawn her to him in the first place. Yes, he was a suave and charming playboy but he was also a man who had firm principles he lived by. His insistence on doing the right thing by Marli was a case in point. He hadn't bolted as soon as he'd known he was to become a father. He had stood by Harper's side and helped her deliver their baby girl. And he had offered to marry her and provide a secure home for their child.

But, as tempting as it was to accept such lifelong security for her child, how could she agree to a loveless marriage? But on the other hand, how could she deny her daughter the full-time presence of a loving and devoted father? Harper wanted her daughter to have everything she hadn't had growing up, and high on that list was a loving father.

But what about what *she* wanted?

Was it wrong to want love for herself? Or was she to be denied it in both childhood and adulthood?

Jack carried Marli in his arms and led Harper out to the hospital car park. Harper glanced at the shiny dark blue luxury model sedan complete with a baby seat in the back. 'This is your car? What happened to the red sports car you had at the Tenterbury wedding?'

'It's back at the hotel. This is what we'll use when taking Marli out and about. It's the safest model on the market.'

Harper had many clients who could afford luxury weddings in exotic locations, but Jack's wealth was on another level. He owned a chain of high-end boutique hotels across the globe. He could buy a brand-new car without flinching at the cost. Harper's business was doing well but she still counted her pennies, every single one of them. A childhood living in poverty made it hard for her to take anything for granted.

'I thought we'd go to the hotel until the house is ready,' Jack said, pressing the remote control that unlocked the car with a musical beep.

'What house?'

'The house I'm in the process of finding for us.'

Harper frowned. 'But I'd like to go back to my flat.'

A steely glint of determination lit his gaze. 'You need support in these early days. And I want to be around Marli as much as possible.'

But that would mean Jack would be around her as well. Hadn't she already betrayed herself by responding to his kiss in the hospital within minutes of giving birth? She had so little immunity to him, especially now with her hormones and emotions all over the place. 'I don't want to live with you, Jack. We're not a couple and—'

'But we are Marli's parents and I don't want my child living in a tiny flat that looks like it could be a fire risk.'

Harper wouldn't admit it to him but she had her own concerns about her flat. The landlord had been lax about some of the repairs that needed doing and some of the other tenants weren't exactly the nicest neighbours to be around. But she had lived in worse dwellings as a child. Far worse. The thought of spending a few days or weeks in a luxury hotel was rather tempting. More than tempting. It would give her time to adjust to being a mother, to get herself in some sort of routine with Marli. But the pay-off was she would be in close contact with Jack Livingstone, the father of her child. Six feet four of arrant masculinity. Oh, joy.

Jack placed Marli in the baby seat with such meticulous care that Harper found it hard to summon up the cynical dislike of him she had taught herself to feel. He wasn't acting like a worldly playboy now, he was acting like a devoted father of a newborn baby girl. But would he revert back to his playboy ways if Harper didn't agree to marry him? Or even if she did marry him? How could she trust a man she didn't really know?

Jack helped Harper into the passenger seat and then pulled down the seat belt for her to clip across her body. 'Are you comfortable?' His blue eyes were shadowed with concern.

'I'm fine.'

He brushed a lazy finger along the curve of her cheek. 'You probably wouldn't admit it if you weren't, would you?'

Harper gave him a self-deprecating glance. 'I'm not used to having people fuss over me.'

'Maybe it's time you had someone do exactly that.' He closed the door and then came around to the driver's side, checking Marli in the back seat first. He opened the driver's door, slid into the seat and, closing the door with a soft snick, sent Harper a probing glance. 'So, what's it to be? Your place or mine?'

Harper raised her eyebrows and sent him a pointed look. 'You're actually giving me a choice?'

He gave a lopsided smile that made something in her belly swoop. 'Kidnapping isn't my modus operandi.'

No, but lethal charm was and she would have to be on her guard to keep herself from falling for it. And falling hard.

They arrived at the flagship Livingstone Hotel a short time later. The uniformed staff at the rear and more private entrance stepped into action. 'Good morning, Mr Livingstone,' one of them greeted Jack with a deferential smile.

'Morning, Ben,' Jack said. 'This is my fiancée, Harper Swan, and this is our daughter, Marli. Please ensure that only my private staff attend to their needs in my suite. And keep the press away. We'll be making a press announcement in a day or two.'

'Certainly, Mr Livingstone.'

Harper waited until Ben was taking her bag out of the boot of the car to speak to Jack. 'Press announcement?'

'I'd like to formally announce Marli's arrival as well as our engagement,' Jack said. 'It's better to be on the front foot rather than having the press chase us for a scoop. That way we control what's said about us.'

The thought of paparazzi chasing her for an exclusive on her relationship with Jack was nothing less than terrifying. She didn't know even know how to describe their relationship. He kept referring to her as his fiancée but she hadn't accepted his proposal…yet. She was starting to waver on it and it scared her because she had always been so adamant about keeping herself free from emotional entanglements that might get in the way of her career. But she hated the thought of robbing Marli of a close relationship with her father. For now, it was easier to run with Jack's plan in order to get through these early weeks of their baby's life. Would the press announce their 'engagement'? What would everyone make of their relationship? She was hardly his normal model-type. She was used to being behind the camera, not in front of it. Her job was to take photos, not to be the subject of them. And she didn't want her baby girl to be hounded by the press, either. But how could she protect her baby when Jack Livingstone was her father? Everyone would want to know about the woman who had given birth to his child. It would be front-page news for sure.

How on earth could she protect her privacy?

A short time later, Jack opened the door of his penthouse suite and Harper stepped inside, trying her best not to be too impressed by the luxury surroundings. The entrance was bigger than her kitchen, the sitting room that came off it bigger than her entire flat. The plush carpet threatened to swallow her up to the knees but the furniture was minimalist and masculine in design, reminding her she had entered Jack's territory. A place where she did not and could not belong.

Marli gave a tiny squawk from the capsule he was carrying and Harper turned to check on her. 'I think she might need changing.'

'I'll do it.' Jack put the capsule down and un-clipped Marli from the fastenings. He took her out and cradled her against his broad chest. 'Where's the changing bag I bought?'

'Here.' Harper handed the bag to him, torn be-tween wanting to watch him with their daughter and needing to keep her distance. He was taking to fatherhood so smoothly, a little more smoothly than she was taking to motherhood—not that she would admit that to anyone. She just needed more time to get used to having a baby. It was all such a shock, an almost traumatic shock in some ways. There was so much responsibility with having a baby. A child was a lifetime's commitment. Harper hadn't even thought about such a commitment, so to suddenly have a baby was profound and emo-tionally unsettling.

Harper found herself following Jack to his bed-room, where he laid Marli on the king-sized bed. He began to undo the press buttons on her little onesie, softly talking to her in his deep, baritone voice. 'I'm going to change your nappy, okay?' He unpeeled the sticky tabs on the nappy and gri-maced. 'Hmm... I think I might need some baby wipes.'

Harper stepped forward and handed them to him. 'Apparently breastfed babies poop a lot.'

'Good to know.' Jack cleaned Marli up and put

on a fresh nappy, and then did the onesie back up. He lifted the baby to his chest again, one of his hands stroking her tiny back. His eyes met Harper's and something in her chest flipped open. 'How are you doing?' There was a gentle note of concern in his voice that was as disarming as his steady, deep blue gaze.

Harper gave a shrug and shifted her gaze from his. 'I'm a bit tired…' She glanced at the bed and then wished she hadn't as a rush of heat flowed through her cheeks. 'Erm, where will I be sleeping?'

'In my bed.'

Harper met his look with a flash of fire in hers. 'Do you really think that's wise?'

His expression was inscrutable. 'There's a fold-out sofa in the sitting room. I'll sleep on that.'

'Oh…' Harper wasn't sure why she should be feeling a pang of disappointment. She didn't want to sleep with him…*did she*? She couldn't sleep with him anyway, not so soon after delivering a baby. It was usual to wait at least four to six weeks before resuming sexual activity. Was there something wrong with her that she desired him even now? That he only had to look at her and her insides would flutter and tighten and coil with lust? That every nerve in her body was acutely, achingly aware of him? That her mouth could still taste the sexy, salty tang of his lips and craved it like a potent drug?

The doorbell of the penthouse suite rang and Harper's gaze flew to Jack's. 'Are you expecting anyone?'

'My mother wants to meet Marli. She's dropping off some presents as well as a bespoke bassinet she insisted on buying for her.'

Harper steeled her gaze and her spine. 'But I don't feel like meeting anyone now, especially someone who's already decided I'm a gold-digger.'

'My mother will adore you once she gets to know you.' Jack went to the door and opened it with Marli still cradled against his chest.

A tall and elegantly dressed woman in her late fifties swept into the room carrying loaded bags. There was a luggage trolley outside the door with a staff member in attendance, and an array of things were stacked on it, including a gorgeous pink and white bassinet. 'Oh, Jack, isn't she just divine?' Liz Livingstone placed the bags on the floor and took the baby from him. 'Oh, look at you, my little darling. You're exactly like your daddy with those big blue eyes. And look at all that hair.' She smothered Marli with kisses, her eyes moist with tears. 'I've waited so long for this moment. I still can't believe it's true. I'm finally a grandmother.'

Jack placed his hand on his mother's shoulder

to turn her to face Harper. 'Mum, this is my fiancée, Harper Swan. Harper, this is my mother, Liz.'

Harper met the older woman's gaze without smiling or speaking. She knew it was rude of her but she was not going to forgive being called a gold-digger in a hurry.

Liz swept her coolly assessing gaze over Harper. 'Well, you're not exactly what I was expecting.'

Harper raised her eyebrows in an imperious manner. 'As you can see, I'm not your son's usual blonde supermodel-type.'

'But you're beautiful for all that.' The compliment was given in a grudging manner by the older woman but Harper refused to be mollified by it. She did not want to get close to Jack or his mother. Jack's mother turning up with a bundle of presents only served to remind Harper of her own mother's absence. Her baby girl had only one grandmother when she should have had two. Liz Livingstone was a protective mother and clearly only wanted what was best for her son. It drove it home even more painfully that Harper had no one looking out for her.

But wasn't that the story of her life?

Marli began to whimper, giving Harper the perfect excuse to take her from Liz's arms. 'Excuse me, I need to feed her.'

It looked for a moment as if Liz wasn't going to

hand the baby over. But then she pursed her lips
and passed Marli to Harper. 'You're feeding her
yourself?'

'Yes.'

'You'll have to weigh her regularly to make sure
she's not losing weight,' Liz said. 'It wouldn't hurt
to give her a bottle or two. That way Jack or I can
feed her.'

Harper held Marli close to her chest, sending
the older woman a challenging glare. 'I don't want
anyone else to feed her but me. And I don't want
her handled by too many strangers.'

'But I'm her grandmother,' Liz said, clearly af-
fronted.

'Mum.' Jack's tone had a note of caution in it.
'We're both still getting over the surprise of having a baby. Take it easy, eh?'

Liz let out a huffy sigh, spun on her heels and
started rummaging in the bags she had brought in.
'All the clothes in here are organic cotton. It's best
for the baby's skin. And I've only bought safety
standard approved toys. You have to be so careful with small beads and batteries and other tiny
things with infants.' She held up a frilly pink outfit. 'Isn't this so cute? I can't wait to dress her in it.'

'We already have enough pink outfits,' Harper
said. 'I want Marli to wear other colours.'

'What? Like black?' Liz said with a scornful roll of her eyes.

The battle lines were drawn, the tension in the air palpable.

'Mum, let's leave Harper to feed Marli in peace,' Jack said on a sigh, taking his mother by the elbow. 'We'll go and have a gin and tonic in the bar downstairs. I'm sure Harper will be happy to see you in a day or two once she's got over the birth.'

'But I want to spend more time with my granddaughter,' Liz insisted. 'I want her to properly bond with me.'

'You'll get plenty of time with her,' Jack said. 'But now's not a good moment.'

'You're damn right it's not,' Harper said under her breath and closed Jack's bedroom door on them both with a resounding click.

CHAPTER SIX

JACK CAME BACK upstairs an hour later once he had seen his mother off. It had taken every one of his negotiating skills and then some to bring his mother around to promising to go slowly with Harper. The last thing he wanted was any animosity between them. He wanted his relationship with Harper to work from the get-go, and any bad feeling on his mother's or Harper's part was not going to do him any favours, nor would it help Marli.

Harper was kneeling in front of the capsule on the floor of the sitting room, rocking it back and forth in a gentle manner. She glanced up at him but went back to staring at their child, her shoulders hunching forward. 'Your mother hates me.'

'Well, you didn't exactly lay on the charm.'

'Why should I? She thinks I'm after your money.'

He scraped a hand through his hair and came over to where she was kneeling. 'You're a mother now, so you'll understand how protective mothers are over their offspring. She just wants what's best for me.'

Harper made a snorting noise. 'Well, clearly that's not me.' She rose to her feet and stood in front of him with a defiant look on her face. 'I can imagine the type of woman she wants you to marry. Someone who comes from an aristocratic background, someone who can move in the circles you move in without embarrassing you.'

'You don't embarrass me,' Jack said, frowning.

She moved past him with a proud toss of her head. 'Yeah? Well, I'm not so sure you won't be embarrassed if the press goes snooping into my background.'

Jack let out a long breath. 'You have no reason to feel ashamed of your background. I know it was tough on you growing up in foster care but look at you now. You're a successful businesswoman.'

Harper picked up a baby blanket and folded it into a neat square, then held it against her body. A flicker of uncertainty passed over her face. 'I'm not sure I can be as successful as I want to be with a baby to look after.'

Jack moved closer and took the blanket from her, placing it on the arm of the nearest sofa. He took her hands in his and was secretly delighted she didn't resist his touch. 'I guess it's a tricky balance for any parent, be they a mother or a father. How do you provide for your family and model a good work ethic while being available and present for your child's needs? It seems almost impossible to get it right.'

Harper lifted her gaze to his. 'Did your mother work or stay at home with you?'

'She stayed at home but sometimes I wish she hadn't.'

'Why?'

Jack released her hands and stepped back. 'My father became ill during my childhood with Parkinson's Disease. She didn't get the chance to resume her career as an architect because my father needed a lot of care, particularly towards the end.'

'Did she want to resume her career?'

'She says not, but she didn't have an easy time with my father,' Jack said. 'He wasn't always difficult, but as the disease progressed he became so. It was tough on her, tougher than she would ever admit, even now. If she'd still had her career, it might have given her an outlet. But my father refused to have anyone but her look after him.'

'I'm sorry to hear that.'

Jack didn't like thinking of just how difficult things had been at times. The sacrifices he and his mother had had to make. The years of hard work to bring things back in the black after his

father's mismanagement. 'I was away at boarding
school by then, so I didn't always see how difficult things were for her or I might have been able
to convince my father to engage the services of a
professional carer. The business began to struggle
and my mother blamed herself for not keeping a
closer eye on things, but it wasn't her area of ex-
pertise, plus my father didn't delegate well. He refused to accept his limitations.'

'I read somewhere you built the business back
up to what it is today,' Harper said. 'But was it
your choice of career?'

No one had ever asked him that question before. Not even his mother. Everyone had assumed
he would gladly follow in his father's footsteps
and take over the hotel business as his father had
done with his own father, Jack's grandfather. The
Livingstone luxury brand was an institution that
could not fail, certainly not on Jack's watch. So,
upon his father's death, Jack had bludgeoned his
own creative dreams into oblivion, determined to
rebuild the family business to honour the legacy
of his grandfather and father. He could not remember the last time he had picked up a paintbrush
and a set of watercolours. It was a part of his life
he had cordoned off like a locked room in a cas-
tle that no longer had a key. 'I would never have

made the money I make today doing anything but what I'm doing.'

'But what did *you* want to do?'

Jack gave an on-off smile to signal the subject was closed and picked up the room service menu. 'I'm going to order some dinner for us. What would you like?'

A short time later, Harper sat at the dining table with Jack. But for once in her life her mind wasn't on food. She kept mulling over the things he had told her about his background. She had always been envious of people who grew up with enormous wealth. They hadn't had to struggle to put food on the table and keep a roof over their head. They hadn't slept under an old coat instead of fine wool blankets or feather and down quilts. But Jack's refusal to discuss his own career aspirations made her wonder if he, like his mother, hadn't been able to pursue his own choice of career due to the responsibilities that fell to his shoulders on his father's illness and then death. Jack had certainly turned the Livingstone Hotel brand into an eye-popping success. There were boutique hotels all over the globe that paid testament to his hard work. The company was one of the most profitable brands in the world and only the rich and famous could afford to stay in a Livingstone Hotel. Which made it highly ironic that she was now living in one with Jack. She wasn't exactly on the poverty line any more but she didn't move in the circles Jack did. If he continued to insist she marry him for the sake of their baby, how would she navigate his world of high-end luxury, of liveried staff and private jets?

'You're not eating,' Jack said. 'Would you like something else? A dessert, perhaps?'

Harper pushed her plate away. 'How do you do it?'

'How do I do what?'

She waved her hand to encompass the luxury suite. 'Live like this? In a hotel, I mean. Don't you feel…a little claustrophobic?'

Jack put his wine glass down on the table. 'I travel so much that I'm only in one place for a night or two.'

Harper picked up her water glass for something to do with her hands. 'Is that why you only have one-night stands?'

His mouth twisted in a rueful manner. 'It suited me to keep things casual.'

'But now?'

His gaze met hers with a directness that was a little unnerving. 'We have a child to raise. We can't be casual about that.'

Harper looked down at the ice cubes in her

water glass. They were slowly melting, becoming one with the mineral water. Was that what was going to happen to her? Her resolve to resist Jack would melt until she couldn't keep herself separate, couldn't live without him? Needing someone was not something she ever wanted to do. Of course, she needed her friends and loved them dearly. But loving a man in a romantic sense had never been on her radar. That was why that night with Jack had been so out of character for her. She had never been so captivated by a man before. She had never been so distracted by a man's charm and banter that she had walked away from her work responsibilities to indulge in a stolen hour or two of toe-curling passion.

Harper looked up from her water glass to meet his gaze once more. 'But you didn't grow up in a hotel, did you?'

'No, we had a home in Buckinghamshire.' He picked up his wine glass again but didn't bring it to his lips. He tilted the glass from side to side, watching as the blood-red wine swirled against the bowl of the glass. 'It was one of the first things we had to sell after my father died. It broke my mother's heart to leave.' He lifted the glass to his lips and took a sip, before putting it down on the table again. His expression gave nothing away but

Harper sensed he too had bitter regrets about losing his family home.

'You haven't tried to buy it back, I mean since?'

Jack's mouth took on a cynical curve. 'No, once I say goodbye to something, that's it. I don't look back.'

'Does that apply to people as well?'

His eyes locked on hers, sending a shiver down her spine. 'I didn't get the chance to say goodbye to you. You slipped out of my hotel room before I woke up. Why was that, hmm?'

Harper could feel a rush of heat flowing into her cheeks at how she had behaved that night. It had been as if she had turned into someone else—a sensual woman who didn't think twice about having casual sex with a stranger. It still shocked her that Jack had distracted her from her work, turning her into a wanton woman who could think of nothing but being in his bed having spine-tingling sex. The sort of sex she had never had before. Sex that was exciting beyond measure. Her body had flown into the stratosphere, trembling, quaking, shuddering with waves of delight she had never experienced with a partner before. Before Jack Livingstone, her pleasure had never been a priority. She had lost count of the number of times she had faked an orgasm to get an encounter over with. But Jack's touch had awakened her in an almost frightening way. She wanted more of him but knew she shouldn't. He was like a forbidden drug she must resist before she became completely addicted. Her mother had fallen for a man she could never have, who had promised but failed to deliver. Jack was promising Harper everything but love. How could she settle for riches and not the most valuable thing of all—love? She lowered her gaze from his probing one and stared at the starched white tablecloth in front of her. 'I wasn't interested in repeating our...hook-up.'

'Because?'

She swallowed tightly, trying not to think of how hard it had been to leave his room when all she had wanted was to stay wrapped in his arms and experience his mind-blowing passion all over again. It had taken an enormous amount of willpower to leave. And it *still* took an enormous amount of willpower to keep her distance from him. Not so easy now she had his baby. They were bound together for the next eighteen years or so whether she liked it or not. She couldn't stop him seeing their child, he wanted to be an involved and loving father, and from all she had seen so far that was exactly what he would be. How could she deny her baby that special relationship? The father-daughter relationship she herself had longed for all her childhood? 'Because I wasn't interested in you.'

'Liar.'

Harper forced her gaze back to his, masking her features into cool impassivity. 'You find it impossible to believe any woman can say no to you, don't you?'

His dark blue eyes kindled with sensual heat. 'You didn't say no. You wanted me as much as I wanted you that night.'

A traitorous drumbeat of lust thrummed in her lower body. Had she no resistance? No immunity to his potent charm? 'That night was a mistake on my part. An aberration.'

Jack glanced to where their baby girl was sleeping in her capsule. 'Is that how you want our daughter to see herself? As a mistake?'

Harper frowned. 'No, of course not. I didn't mean it like that.'

There was a pulsing silence.

'If you had found out about the pregnancy earlier, what would you have done?' Jack asked.

Harper chewed at her lower lip, not quite able to meet his gaze. 'I'm not sure what you're asking…'

'Would you have told me? Or simply had a termination?'

She brought her gaze back to his. 'I don't think there are too many women who consider having a termination a simple solution. It's a big decision to make, and not one I would have liked to make, although I respect other people's reasons for doing so.' She paused for a beat and continued, 'I would have told you, though. I would have given you the choice to be involved or not.'

Jack's gaze drifted back to their sleeping baby, his expression cast in lines of awe that tugged on Harper's heart strings. He loved his child; did that mean he might one day fall in love with her? 'I can't imagine not being involved now she's here.' Marli opened her tiny mouth and yawned, one of her little starburst hands stretching above her head. Jack shifted his gaze back to Harper's, his expression turning serious. 'I wouldn't have pressured you into having a termination. I firmly believe it's a woman's choice what happens to her body.'

Harper gave him a pointed look. 'But here you are, pressuring me into marrying you.'

His mouth went into a tight line. 'It's the best possible solution to our situation. It will provide security and stability for Marli and you going forward.'

Security and stability were the two words that were foremost in Harper's mind at the best of times, even more so now she had a baby to consider. But would marrying a man she barely knew be the best possible solution? A man she had suppressed her feelings for out of a sense of imminent danger. A man who only had to touch her and she erupted into flames of rabid lust. Marrying Jack Livingstone might provide her daughter with a loving and present father but it would provide Harper with a temptation she wasn't sure she could resist.

And she suspected Jack knew it.

A couple of days later, Ruby and Aerin arranged to call in to meet Marli. As it turned out, Jack had to see to a work issue at one of his hotels in Edinburgh, so was away from early in the morning to catch a flight to Scotland.

'Oh, look at her, isn't she gorgeous?' Aerin said, melting at the sight of Marli dressed in a duckling-yellow outfit Jack had brought back home the day before.

'You're making me seriously clucky,' Ruby said, with a smile. She turned to look at Harper. 'How are you managing? It must be such a huge change.'

Harper gave a shrug. Should she tell her friends how uncertain she was about everything? Should she admit to the fears that stalked her? Fears about not succeeding with her career. Fears about not being a good enough mother. Fears about never being truly loved by her baby's father. How could she admit to such insecurities without worrying her friends? New motherhood was supposed to be a happy, if not euphoric, time. Instead, she was struggling with a host of conflicting emotions. She loved her baby, of course she did. But she was worried she might become overwhelmed the way her mother had become, the burden of motherhood too much, especially without a man who loved her by her side. 'I'm coping.'

Ruby leaned closer and placed a gentle hand on Harper's arm, her expression etched with concern. 'Only just coping?'

Harper let out a ragged sigh. 'I haven't been out of the hotel since I got here. Yesterday, I didn't have a shower until three in the afternoon. I used to be so organised and now I'm not sure what I'm doing or even if I'm doing it correctly. I worry Marli isn't getting enough milk, then I worry she isn't sleeping or sleeping too much. I didn't realise there was so much to worry about.'

'Oh, you poor darling,' Aerin said, making a sympathetic moue with her mouth. 'You haven't had time to prepare for motherhood. Most pregnant women spend the entire nine months planning and preparing and reading up on it. You were suddenly thrust into all this without notice. No wonder you're feeling a little out of your depth. Anyone would feel the same.'

'Isn't Jack helping you?' Ruby asked.

'Yes, he's been great, but he had to fly to Edinburgh to one of his hotels today. I'm not sure what time he'll be back. He didn't say.' Which kind of summed up their relationship. A come-and-go, fly-in, fly-out arrangement. Jack might insist on marrying her for Marli's sake, but it wasn't a true partnership.

Aerin was still cuddling Marli, moving from side to side in a rocking motion to soothe her back to sleep. 'Why don't you have a shower now and we'll head out for a walk in the sunshine? It's a gorgeous day and the fresh air will be good for Marli. We can grab some lunch and we can mind Marli while you get your hair or nails done. You'll feel like a new woman in no time.'

Within an hour, Harper was sitting at an outdoor café with her three friends, enjoying a late lunch. It was almost like being back to normal, except the responsibility of her baby made her conscious of the change in the dynamic with her friends. How could she fulfil her commitments as a wedding photographer when she was nursing a baby? She didn't want to compromise her bonding with Marli but neither did she want to inconvenience her friends. They had solid bookings for weddings and finding a fill-in photographer was not as easy as it sounded, especially finding one with the high creative standards that matched their business model.

It was amazing how many people coming in and out of the café—mostly women but even occasionally a man who was a new father himself—stopped to comment on Marli. The gushing comments on how cute she was, how adorable her outfit, how tiny she was, couldn't help but make Harper feel proud. Her body had produced this perfect little being, a gorgeous little baby who had come into the world in the most surprising and unexpected way, and yet Harper's love for her was automatic and complete. If only Jack's love for *her* was as automatic and complete as it was for their child.

But just as Harper was packing up to leave with her friends, another person came rushing over and Harper looked up to see none other than Clara Tenterbury, the bride from the society wedding where Harper had spent the night with Jack. Her stomach dropped, her mouth fell open, her mind went totally blank.

'Oh, my God!' Clara squealed. 'What a little poppet. How old is she? She is a she, right?'

Harper was not used to being struck dumb, but trying to explain her circumstances to Clara Tenterbury was beyond her capabilities right then. Maybe there was such a thing as baby brain, for her brain did feel a little scrambled. What twist of fate had led Clara to be at the same café as Harper and her friends? 'Erm…' Harper began but couldn't get her voice to complete the sentence, couldn't get her mind to even form a sentence to say.

'This is Marli Elizabeth Susannah Swan-Livingstone,' Aerin said, with a proud aunty-like smile. 'Isn't she absolutely gorgeous?'

Clara's eyes bulged like oversized marbles. 'Did you say… *Livingstone*? As in Jack Livingstone?'

Aerin bit her lip and glanced at Harper with a worried oops-I-think-I made-a-boo-boo look on her face. Harper was thinking of how many followers Clara had on social media. Thousands, possibly millions by now. It had been a positive thing for her and her business partners when Clara had gushed about how wonderfully they had done her wedding to Hugh Tenterbury. But now? It was a potential nightmare.

Harper fixed a stiff smile on her face. 'How are you, Clara? Enjoying married life?' What else could she do but deflect? There was no way she was going into the details of Marli's conception. No freaking way.

Clara's eyes danced. 'Wonderful.' She placed a hand on her own abdomen. 'I have my own exciting news to share. Hugh and I are expecting a baby. A boy. Hugh is so ridiculously proud. I bet Jack is too.'

After the appropriate congratulations were

given, Ruby came to the rescue and diverted the conversation away from Harper by chatting about where Clara and Hugh had gone for their honeymoon, telling her of her own plans for her wedding to Lucas Rothwell. And within a few minutes Clara was gone, giving them all a fingertip wave on the way out.

Harper blew out a ragged breath and passed Marli to Ruby to hold, so she could pack up her things. 'Thanks, Ruby, for rescuing me. I thought she would never leave.'

'That's okay,' Ruby said. 'I could see you were a bit stuck for words.'

'I'm so sorry,' Aerin said, still looking worried about her gaffe.

'Don't worry about it,' Harper reassured her. 'I couldn't think how to explain about my cryptic pregnancy without looking like a complete idiot.' It was hard not to feel a little envious of Clara, who was clearly enjoying every moment of her pregnancy. How had she not known her own body was undergoing the same changes? It still didn't make sense…or did it? Had her mind switched into a pattern of denial so strong it had prevented her from seeing what was right in front of her?

Ruby looked down at the baby in her arms with a wistful expression on her face. 'Marli's like a little angel. I still can't believe none of us suspected you were pregnant.' She glanced up at Harper. 'Did you even for a moment think you might be?'

Harper was about to say 'no' but then realised it wasn't strictly true. There had been odd moments when the thought had crossed her mind but not for long enough to take a firm hold. 'I've been thinking about that… I was late the first month but only by a few days. Then I had sore breasts for a week or two, but then I sometimes do before a period. And I had a lighter than normal period a few times.' She frowned and continued, 'I think I might have been in denial, so couldn't allow the thought any traction in my head. I feel such a fool now, though. How could I not have realised on some level?'

'Denial is a powerful tool when we don't want to face stuff we need to face,' Ruby said. 'But it all turned out in the end. Marli is perfect and you and Jack are going to be wonderful parents. You're lucky he wants to be involved. Just like for you, it must have been an incredible shock for him.'

'But what if the novelty wears off?' Harper asked. 'Marli is cute now but babies grow bigger and get noisy and messy and hard to control. He might not feel so committed to her once she's a defiant toddler or a moody teenager.'

'But even some mothers can feel ambivalent towards their kids,' Ruby said with a rueful twist to her mouth. 'My mother being a case in point. Jack might prove to be the best father you could ask for your little girl. You have to give him a chance to prove himself.'

'By marrying him?' Harper asked. 'How can I marry a man who doesn't love me? Who doesn't even believe in the concept of long-lasting love?'

'Playboys always say that until they fall in love themselves,' Ruby said with a dreamy smile. 'Just ask Lucas.'

'And my father,' Aerin said with a grin. 'You should have heard his soppy speech about Mum at their wedding anniversary weekend. There wasn't a dry eye in the house, not even his.'

But Harper wasn't so sure she could hold on to the hope that Jack might fall in love with her one day. What if he didn't? What if their marriage became a cold and clinical arrangement that left them both unsatisfied and their child had to grow up witnessing it?

CHAPTER SEVEN

JACK RETURNED TO his penthouse later that day to find Harper and Marli were not there. He went from room to room, trying to quell the panic rising like a toxic tide in his chest. Surely she wouldn't have left without informing him? But her absence brought back the memory of that night nine months ago, waking to find her gone, only the indentation of her head on the pillow next to his. The frustration he had felt shocked him then as it shocked him now. He hadn't been expecting her to do a runner. He was offering her much more now than a simple fling. He was offering marriage and a secure future for her and their child. Why would she leave without at least telling him where she was going? Marli was his child too, so he had a right to know where she was and if she was safe.

The door opened behind him and he swung around to see Harper coming in carrying Marli in a front pouch strapped to her chest. 'You're back,' she said, closing the door behind her with the kick of her left foot.

'Where the hell have you been?' Jack asked. 'I was worried about you. You didn't tell me you were going out.'

Harper's dark eyebrows rose ever so slightly over her eyes in an unmistakably haughty manner. 'Am I supposed to check in and out with you on my every movement?'

Jack let out a rough-edged breath. 'No, I was just expecting you to be here when I got back. You didn't call or even send a text.'

She slipped the straps of the carrier from her shoulders, her other hand cupping the baby's bottom to hold her steady against her. 'I went out with Aerin and Ruby. We had lunch and they looked after Marli while I got my hair and nails done. Not that I should have to explain myself to you. Last time I looked I was a free agent.'

Jack had to stop himself from pacing the floor in frustration. He couldn't get his panic back in its box. His worries over her and Marli's safety were new things to deal with, new concerns to add to his list of responsibilities. Responsibilities he took seriously. 'But what if the press saw you?'

Harper's gaze hardened to steel but there was a hint of pink in her cheeks, suggesting she might have already thought of the possibility of being exposed. 'So that's what worried you? That I might leak something to the press about us?'

'Don't be ridiculous, that's not what I meant at all. I want to make an announcement about us on my terms. It's important our relationship is seen as the real deal for Marli's sake.' He rubbed the back of his neck, where a knot of tension had built since he left that morning. The hotel management meeting hadn't gone as well as he would have liked. He had tried to focus to problem-solve the issues but he had been completely distracted, wanting to be back with Harper and the baby. It was so out of character for him not to put work first. To narrow his focus so nothing else existed. He had even pressed a pause button on the meeting so he could go out and buy an engagement ring at an exclusive jewellery store he had heard about from a colleague.

Harper laid the baby down in the bassinet and tucked the bunny blanket around her. She turned and glanced at him, her eyes still glittering with ire. 'I've been stuck in this hotel room for days. I needed to get out for some fresh air. Sorry if that doesn't meet with your approval but I can't stay hidden up here like a dirty little secret.'

Jack released another long-winded sigh and came over to her, taking her hands in his. 'You surely don't see yourself as that?'

Her gaze slipped out of reach of his, one of her slim shoulders rising and falling in a shrug. 'I can only imagine what the press will make of me once they hear about us. Your mother already thinks I'm a gold-digger, so I can only assume others will too.'

Jack tipped up her chin with his finger, locking her gaze on his. 'Not once we formalise our relationship.' He released her hands to take the jewellery box out of his trouser pocket. He handed it to her. 'I hope it fits. I had to guess your ring size.'

She hesitated for a moment, then took the square velvet box from his open palm as if it contained something dangerous. She gingerly prised open the lid and gasped at the princess cut diamond. 'Jack…it's too much. It must've cost a fortune.' She frowned up at him. 'It's such a beautiful ring for a loveless commitment such as ours.'

He took the ring out of the box and slid it along her ring finger, immensely relieved it fitted her perfectly. Was that an omen or what? But so much about Harper fitted him perfectly. Her sensuality was unmatched. He could not remember a lover who had thrilled him the way she had. 'We love our baby, that's all that matters for now.' He took her hand and brought it up to his mouth, pressing his lips against the ring and then each of her fingertips in turn.

Her gaze drifted to his mouth and her slim throat rose and fell over a swallow. Uncertainty shadowed her grey-green gaze. 'Marriage is such a big step...'

Jack placed one of his hands against the curve of her cheek, his thumb stroking the smooth skin of her face in a slow-motion caress. 'We'll be good together.'

She ran the tip of her tongue over her pillowy lips and a drumbeat of lust thrummed in his groin. Was it his imagination or had she leaned closer to him? He placed his other hand on her right hip, easing her closer, his body on fire as soon as her pelvis came into contact with his. She snatched in an audible breath and her gaze focused back on his mouth. 'Jack...' Her voice was little more than a whisper, a husky, sexy whisper that sent a frisson down his spine.

Jack lowered his mouth to hers, taking his time, allowing her the chance to pull back if she didn't want to go any further. But instead of pulling away, she moved forward as if drawn to him by an invisible force—the same invisible force that was driving him towards her. Their lips met in a feather-light touchdown, once, twice, three times. But instead of quelling the need for sensual contact, it fuelled it.

Fervently. Fiercely. Ferociously.

Her mouth came back to his in a kiss that was as hot as fire, the pressure of her lips sending his senses reeling. She opened her mouth beneath the increasingly urgent pressure of his, their tongues tangling in a dance as old as time. Jack knew it was too soon to take things any further, but somehow, knowing they could only kiss and caress for now intensified the contact. It brought something new and exciting to each movement of their lips against each other's. A sweet poignancy that plucked at something deep in his chest, something he had never felt with anyone else. Her mouth was sweet and soft and yet exotic, her tongue playful and yet determined. Her arms wound around his neck, holding him closer, her full breasts crushed against his chest.

Jack lifted his mouth from hers to blaze a pathway of hot kisses down from below her ear to the scaffolding of her collarbone. Her soft, breathless sounds of encouragement and pleasure sent shivers of delight through him. The chemistry between them on their first encounter nine months ago had stunned him then and it stunned him now. How could a simple kiss, a caress, a breathless murmur of pleasure send his pulse skyrocketing?

Jack shifted his mouth to the delicate shell of her ear, breathing in the scent of her freshly washed hair, which tickled his face. He swept it back over her shoulder, placing his mouth on the side of her neck, his tongue teasing the soft, creamy skin. 'You taste so damn delicious, I think I'm getting addicted to you,' he growled deep in his throat.

Harper gave a delicate shudder and lifted one of her hands to his face, sliding it down the rough, late-in-the-day stubble. 'We shouldn't be doing this…' Her voice was still whisper-soft, her eyes dark and lustrous as wet paint.

'We're only kissing,' Jack said. 'It's too soon for anything else.'

A faint blush pooled in her cheeks and she lowered her gaze to his mouth. Her fingertip traced the outline of his lips and every nerve reacted to her sensual touch, making him hot and tight and hard as stone. He recalled how she used those clever little fingertips on his body, tiptoeing all over him, teasing him all those months ago, pleasuring him with her lips and tongue and taking him to heaven and beyond.

Jack brought his mouth back down to hers and she sighed against his lips, her arms going around his neck again. Her fingers played with the hair brushing his collar, sending shivers of reaction down the length of his spine. She eased back from his mouth to glance up at him with a slightly dazed expression on her face. 'I don't think I've ever been kissed like that before.' She circled his mouth with her finger again, slowly, tantalisingly.

Jack captured her hand and pressed a warm kiss to her open palm, teasing the skin with a poke of his tongue, watching as her pupils flared in desire. 'Nor have I,' he said and kissed her again.

Harper knew it was dangerous to kiss Jack. Dangerous and addictive, but how could she help herself? He triggered a need in her that was so strong it overrode every other thought in her brain. All she wanted was the taste and texture of his mouth on hers, the sweep and glide and sexy thrust of his tongue in her mouth that made her blood sing and tap dance in her veins. It didn't seem possible that she could feel such a powerful rush of desire so soon after having a baby. But that was Jack Livingstone's power over her. He was able to undo her physically like no one else.

Jack finally released her with a rueful sigh. 'I'd better stop before I get carried away. Besides, you need your rest. Why don't you put your feet up while I check on Marli?'

'Okay.' It piqued Harper that it was Jack who was the first to break the sensual interlude. Why hadn't she stepped back first? Why hadn't she shown him she could resist him? Why hadn't she had the willpower to keep him at arm's length?

Because she didn't have the willpower. She never had.

Would she ever?

A couple of days later, Harper was having breakfast with Jack before he left for the office, when one of Jack's staff informed him via the intercom his mother was asking to come up.

Harper frowned and put down her cup of tea with a clatter against the saucer. 'But it's seven-thirty in the morning. Why can't she come at a reasonable hour?'

Jack put his napkin on the table and pushed back his chair. 'She hasn't seen Marli since we first brought her home from hospital. She's waited years to be a grandmother. Indulge her. Being a grandmother will make up for all the things she had to sacrifice for my father. It will give her a purpose again.'

Harper understood Jack wanted his mother involved in his daughter's life. She knew the value of grandparents even though she hadn't experienced it for herself. Ruby, for instance, had been reared by her grandmother and spoke lovingly of the memories of growing up at Rothwell Park, where her grandmother was the housekeeper to Lucas's family. Aerin still had both sets of grandparents and also spoke positively about the joy of being in-

dulged and thoroughly spoilt by the older generation. Harper glanced down at her nightgown and
wrap. She had been up a lot during the night, feeding Marli and feeling like a zombie. Jack had got
up each time with her, but despite the interrupted
sleep he looked disgustingly fresh after a shower
and a shave. 'But I'm not dressed for visitors.'

'Why don't you make use of her while she's
here?' He flicked his shirt sleeve back to check his
designer watch. 'I have to get to an early meeting
in a few minutes. Mum can mind Marli while you
have a shower or even go back to bed for a bit.'

Jack went to let his mother into the penthouse
and Harper sat fuming. The last thing she wanted
to do was entertain Jack's mother, even if she was
a devoted grandmother.

Liz came into the dining room with a newspaper tucked under her arm, her expression etched
in lines of disapproval. 'I suppose we have you to
thank for this.' She tossed the tabloid newspaper
on the table in front of Harper.

Harper looked down at the photo of her holding
Marli at the café with Aerin and Ruby the other
day. Her heart came to a jerky standstill, a cold
shiver crawling over her scalp like the march of
ice-footed ants. The headline read: *Wedding Photographer and Former Foster Child Harper Swan
Has Secret Love-Child with Billionaire Hotelier*

Jack Livingstone. Her eyes ran over the rest of the article detailing snippets of information about Jack and herself, most of which were fabricated. Surely Clara Tenterbury hadn't fed the press such sensationalist rubbish? Harper glanced up at Jack, whose expression was as frozen as a marble statue. 'Jack, you can't possibly think *I* was behind this?'

His dark blue gaze was hard and cynical. 'Can't I?'

'I warned you, Jack,' Liz Livingstone said. 'This is exactly what I was saying about—'

'Mum, please leave this to me,' Jack said in a clipped tone. 'Go and check on Marli. She's in the bedroom.'

His mother pursed her lips, pulled back her shoulders, turned on her heels and stalked out.

Harper pushed the paper away, nauseated by the thought of millions of people speculating about her. She stood from the table, wrapping her arms around her middle, her pulse thudding in panic and distress. 'I didn't do this, Jack. I would never speak to the press.'

'Clearly someone did. One of your friends?'

'No, Aerin and Ruby would never betray me like that.' She moistened her dry-as-toast lips and continued, 'When we had lunch the other day we ran into Clara Tenterbury. I know she and Hugh are your friends but she's the only one who could have done this. She was fascinated to see me holding a baby. I couldn't think of a thing to say. I didn't know how to explain our situation. But Aerin told her Marli's full name, which of course included your surname hyphenated with mine. Clara then jumped on that and, well, I guess that's what led to this.' She jerked her head towards the newspaper on the table as if it were a poisonous spider.

Jack snatched up the paper, screwed it up and then tossed it in the nearest bin. His expression was thunderous, stark lines of tension running either side of his mouth. 'I wanted to control what was said about us in the press. I planned to make an announcement as soon as we agreed on a wedding date.' He scraped a hand down his face, momentarily distorting his handsome features. He lowered his hand and let out a harsh-sounding breath. 'God, what a freaking mess.'

'Do you believe me?' Harper tried not to sound too desperate for his trust but she needed him to believe her. She of all people knew what it was to be lied to or about, which was why she had a reputation for being honest to the point of bluntness. The only person she ever lied to was herself. But that was something she didn't want to think about right now. Her feelings for Jack, the feelings she tried so hard to squash, were still throbbing away inside her, aching to find a way out of the prison she had locked them in.

Jack came over to her and took her left hand, running his thumb over the diamond he had put there the day she had met with her friends. His eyes meshed with hers, his mouth tilted in a grim smile. 'If you say you didn't do it, then of course I believe you. Anyone could have taken that photo or overheard you talking with Clara and your friends. I'll release my own announcement today.'

Sudden moisture prickled at the backs of her eyes, two tears escaping in spite of her best efforts to hold them back. Jack reached up with his other hand and blotted them with his fingertip, his expression softened with concern. 'Do you want me to send my mother away? I don't like leaving you alone when you're upset but I have an important meeting I can't cancel at short notice. I'll explain what's happened to her. I'm sure she'll understand.'

Harper stepped out of his embrace and painted a stiff smile on her face. 'I'm fine. No, don't send her away. She's the only grandmother Marli has, and it's only right she gets to spend time with her.'

Jack touched her gently on the back of her hand, a light grazing of his fingertips that sent a frisson through her body. 'How does September 1st sound for a wedding day?'

Harper had never pictured herself as a bride. She wasn't like her friends and clients who had dreamed since childhood of finding true love and riding off into the sunset with their soulmate. She was far too practical, too committed to her career to hanker after the happy-ever-after so many others longed to find. But she had a baby to consider now, a child who had the right to be involved with her father. A father who promised to love and provide for Marli. How could Harper deny her little girl the security she herself had longed for but never experienced growing up? 'That's only two months away,' she said.

'Will that be a problem?'

The only problem was the fact Jack would be marrying her without being in love with her. And didn't most brides long for that more than anything else?

'Lucas and Ruby's wedding is in late October. I don't want to disrupt their plans by squeezing in our wedding before theirs. A wedding takes weeks if not months to plan. I don't want to take the attention off them and put it on us. Can't we wait until I get back from Paris to decide on a date?'

Jack let out a sigh of resignation. 'Okay, but I don't believe in long engagements.'

He didn't believe in love either and that was Harper's biggest problem of all.

* * *

Jack left after speaking to his mother, and a few minutes later Harper went in to where Liz was seated in the bedroom, holding Marli in her arms. The baby was looking up at her grandmother and Liz was cooing to her in a sing-song voice that made Harper realise how much she had missed out on by not having had a grandmother herself. Liz Livingstone might not approve of her son's choice of bride but no one could question her adoration of her infant granddaughter.

Liz looked up as Harper stood framed in the door. 'I hope Jack isn't making a big mistake in marrying you. I've always wanted him to marry for love.'

Harper adopted a don't-mess-with-me expression, curling her top lip for good measure. 'How do you know he doesn't love me?'

Liz's chin went up to an imperious height. 'He told me so.'

Harper had to work hard not to show how much the older woman's words wounded her. It was like being struck in the face with a blunt object, the pain travelling to every part of her body in stinging, pulsating waves. Surely Jack could have at least *pretended* to love her for the sake of appearances? Was she to suffer the shame and indignity of always being seen as not good enough?

Not worthy enough?

Unlovable? But hadn't she always believed that about herself?

Harper pushed herself away from where she was leaning indolently against the door jamb. 'He might not love me but look at the size of the ring he gave me. Pretty awesome, huh?' She knew she was acting exactly like the trashy little gold-digger Jack's mother thought her to be, but right then she didn't care.

The older woman's mouth tightened like the strings of an old-fashioned purse, her eyes flashing with loathing. 'I don't believe for a moment you didn't set Jack up by deliberately falling pregnant. You saw him as a meal ticket and went for it with both greedy hands. Cryptic pregnancy be damned. You might have convinced everyone else but you haven't convinced me.'

'If you have an issue with me falling pregnant, you'd best speak to your son,' Harper shot back with venom. 'They were his condoms, not mine.'

Liz's cheeks burned a deep shade of pink as if the intimate topic was way outside of her normal experience. 'I only hope you turn out to be a better mother to Marli than you'll be a wife to my son.'

Harper locked gazes with Jack's mother as if she was in a boxing tournament and determined at all costs to win. 'I damn well will be.'

CHAPTER EIGHT

Four weeks later...

JACK CAME IN from a long day, after being in Rome for an important meeting, to find Harper asleep on the sofa in front of the television. The volume was so low he didn't see the point of having it on at all but he guessed she was trying not to disturb Marli, who was usually asleep at this time in the bedroom.

He hunkered down in front of Harper, gently stroking his fingers through her hair. He found it increasingly hard to keep himself from touching her. The magnetic pull had only intensified over the last month. The sensual energy between them was at times palpable. If ever she touched him even incidentally—such as when she was passing him Marli—a lightning-fast zap of energy shot through his blood. And it was obvious she felt the same, for she often pulled her hand back, or blushed, or turned away as if to disguise her reaction.

'Hey, sleepyhead. Wouldn't you be more comfortable in bed?'

Harper opened her eyes and blinked owlishly at him. 'What time is it?' Her voice was soft and slurry from sleep.

'Half one in the morning.'

She groaned and pulled herself up to a sitting position, her long, sleep-tousled hair tumbling about her shoulders. 'How was your trip to…where did you go again?' She scrunched up her face as if trying to recall their conversation earlier that morning.

Jack sat beside her, resting one of his arms along the back of the sofa. 'Rome.'

'Oh, that's right. Sorry, my memory is all over the place.'

He threaded his fingers through her hair again, loving the silky feel of it against his skin,the fruity fragrance of it filling his senses and making him want to bury his face against her neck and breathe in more of her. She didn't move away from his touch, but instead leaned into it, her eyes closing momentarily, like a cat that was blissfully enjoying being stroked.

'It's because you don't get enough sleep.'

She opened her eyes and turned her head to

meet his gaze. 'Nor do you. Do you normally work such long hours? And travel so much?'

Jack had actively sought time away to process what was happening between them. What was happening to him. Feelings he refused to acknowledge, feelings he didn't want to name or examine in any detail were burgeoning inside him. Spending day after day with Harper made it near impossible to keep his heart off limits. He wasn't sure what it was about her that chipped away at his emotional armour so relentlessly. But strangely, time away from her didn't help at all. It only made him miss her and Marli all the more. He threw himself into his work with a passion he didn't feel. The only passion he had was for Harper.

Jack let out a long sigh and reached for one of her hands, holding it between both of his. 'There are a few new developments I'm juggling right now. Plus, the house I'm in the process of buying needs some work. I want everything perfect before we move in with Marli.'

'You sound like Aerin. She's such a perfectionist, which is what makes her such a brilliant wedding planner.'

'How are your friends managing without you?'

Her slim shoulders went up and down in a shrug. 'Okay, I guess… They've found a photographer but she can only cover the next couple of months. It's so hard on Aerin and Ruby without me there. We're a team and we complement each other so well. I feel like I've created a logistical nightmare for them.'

He stroked the back of her hand with a lazy finger. 'You really miss work, don't you?'

She gave him a worried look. 'Does that make me a bad mother?'

'Of course not.' He brought her hand up to his mouth, pressing a kiss to her bent knuckles, his gaze meshed with hers. 'You're good at what you do and you're not used to having a break this long from doing it. But we'll be in Paris soon for your photo shoot, so hopefully that will make you feel more in touch with your work. And we can look at engaging a nanny if you—'

Harper pulled her hand out of his and frowned. 'I don't want a nanny.'

'But you were the one who first suggested it.'

She lowered her gaze, her frown still visible on her forehead. 'Like foster parents, nannies come and go. I don't want that for Marli. I want her to experience stability and security. I don't want her passed around like a parcel no one really wants.'

Jack knew Harper carried a lot of emotional scars from her childhood. Even the most normal and loving childhoods still left wounds that often took a lifetime to heal. How much harder must it have been for her, never having a father invested in her and losing her mother so young. It was amazing she had made such a success of her life to date. Many people did not.

'But we're going to have to do something because we both have big careers. What about asking my mother? I'm sure she'd be happy to help.'

Harper bounced off the sofa as if propelled by an ejector button. Her arms went around her middle, her expression stormy. 'I don't feel comfortable around your mother. She's always on her best behaviour when you're around, but she can be so annoying when you're not. She hasn't shut up about that stupid press release.'

Jack rose from the sofa and came over to her, placing his hands on her shoulders. 'I dealt with the press release by officially announcing our engagement.'

Her gaze met his with a diamond-hard glitter. 'But we're not in love and that upsets your mother. She can't bear the thought of her only son marrying someone he knocked up after a one-night stand.'

His hands fell away from her shoulders and he let out a jagged sigh. 'My mother comes from a different generation, in some ways even older and more traditional than the one she was born into. The thought of sleeping with someone just for sex is foreign to her. My father was her only lover and she remained faithful to him for life.'

'Did your father stay faithful to her?'

The question blindsided Jack for a moment. There was so much he didn't know about his father due to how his illness had ravaged him over the years. And because he had been away at boarding school for a lot of that time, there hadn't been too many father-son bonding sessions to be had, even had his father been into that sort of thing.

'That's something I can't answer because I didn't ask and he didn't say,' Jack said. 'We didn't have a particularly close relationship. If we had, he might have told me of the difficulties he was having keeping our finances in order.'

Harper's expression softened into shades of compassion. 'It must have been a terrible shock to find things weren't as in order as you expected.'

Jack gave a grunt of agreement. 'Yeah, it was. I had to do a business degree and Masters in record time to turn things around. It hit my mother hard too. She had to adjust to not only life without my father but also the lifestyle she was accustomed to. And, of course, she had no career to fall back on, having given up so much to look after him.' His mouth twisted in a rueful grimace. 'I think that's why she can be so pedantic and controlling now. She doesn't want to get caught out again.'

Harper stepped closer to him and placed a hand on his forearm. His skin tingled and tightened at her touch and a wave of smouldering heat flowed through his body. 'I'll try and be a little more accommodating towards her, for Marli's sake, as well as yours.' Her voice had a husky edge that sent a shiver along his nerve endings.

Jack placed his hands on her hips and held her just apart from his body. The desire to bring her flush against him was almost uncontrollable. Her gaze went to his mouth, stayed there for a beat or two, then she glanced up at him again.

'Jack...?' This time her voice was barely audible, a soft, breathless whisper that seemed to contain a beseeching plea.

He tilted up her chin to keep her gaze locked on his. 'What else is troubling you?'

She gave a lopsided smile and lifted her hand to his face, gliding it down the length of his jaw. 'You trouble me, more than I care to admit.'

'In what way?'

'This way,' she said, and, stepping on tiptoe, planted a soft-as-a-puff-of-air kiss to his lips. But, for all its lightness, her kiss still sent a shockwave of fiery lust through him.

Jack brought her closer to his body, close enough to feel every sweet curve of her against his hardening flesh. He brought his mouth down to hers in a kiss that set off fireworks in his blood. She opened her lips to welcome the stroke and glide of his tongue and a hot shiver rolled down his spine. She tasted of milk and honey and something that was uniquely her. The taste he had craved for months like a drug he couldn't resist. His tongue duelled with hers in an erotic game that made the hairs on his head lift away from his scalp. Her soft little moans of pleasure and encouragement thrilled him, excited him, fuelled him to kiss her deeper, harder, more insistently.

He raised his mouth from hers, his breathing already ragged. 'Isn't it too soon to be doing this?'

Her arms snaked around his neck, her full breasts crushed against his chest. 'I had my postnatal check-up today. I've been given the go-ahead to do whatever I like.'

Jack framed her face in his hands, looking deeply into her eyes. 'Are you sure this is what you want? It's late, you're lacking sleep. You might see it differently in the morning.'

She lifted her hand to his mouth, tracing its outline with a teasing stroke of her finger. 'It *is* already morning. Don't you want to see if what we experienced all those months ago was just a fluke or…something else?'

It had certainly been something else—something outside of Jack's not inconsiderable wealth of experience. The sensual energy between them had thrown him into nine months of self-imposed celibacy. He hadn't wanted to wipe out the memory of her touch with someone else's. He couldn't understand why she was the one woman to have such an effect on him. He had slept with plenty of beautiful women but none had left a lingering need in him to see them again and again and again. Harper had put a roadblock up, which he had to accede had only intensified his determination to have her in the end. He was used to women chasing him. It was a refreshing change to be the pursuer rather than the pursued.

Jack's hands tightened on her hips, his need for her building to the point of pain. 'Yes, I do, but I don't think it was a fluke. You turn me on like no one else.'

But then a tiny squawking cry sounded from the bedroom. 'Waa-waa-waa.'

Harper sagged against him wearily with a sigh. 'I'd better go to her. She's due for a feed in half an hour anyway.'

Jack gave her one quick kiss before he released her. He suppressed his disappointment because he knew their little baby had to come first. He wouldn't have it any other way—Marli was his top priority, which was why it was so frustrating Harper was still so adamant about waiting until after Ruby and Lucas's wedding to decide on a wedding date. He considered making her wait to resume a sexual relationship with him until after that, but that would mean another two months of torture. Never had he wanted someone as much as he wanted her. It didn't mean he was falling in love. He would never allow his heart to get involved to that degree. He admired her, liked her, respected her and desired her.

And he couldn't see that changing anytime soon, if ever.

Harper fed and changed Marli and settled her back to sleep. She returned to the sitting room to find Jack in the same position he had found her in an hour before. He was lying on his side, his head resting on the same scatter cushion she had used. He was still dressed in his business shirt and trousers but he had taken off his shoes and socks. His black hair was sexily tousled and there was a generous sprinkling of dark stubble on his jaw. She went over to him and perched on the edge of the sofa next to his hip. Every cell in her body ached to touch him, to lean down and press a hot kiss to his mouth, to stir him into wakefulness and arousal.

But something stopped her.

Was she making a mistake by wanting to make love to him again? By wanting to revisit the mind-blowing passion they had shared that had resulted in the conception of their tiny baby? Jack wanted to marry her but not for the reasons most people got married. He desired her—she was in no doubt of that—but was it enough to last a lifetime together? Or even last enough years for them to successfully raise their child?

As if by its own volition, her hand reached out and lightly touched his lean jaw. The prickle of his stubble tickled her fingers but apart from a sleepy murmur, he didn't wake. He had been in and out of the country several times since Marli's birth, always flying back the same day, juggling work and fatherhood with his many other commitments. Like hers, his life had changed in a blink. One day he was a billionaire playboy hotelier who flew around the globe to maintain the success of his hotel brand, the next he was a devoted father, trying to be present and engaged in every aspect of Marli's care. It could have been so different. He might not have wanted anything to do with their baby. He could have left Harper to deal with everything on her own but he hadn't. He had promised to marry her, to provide for and protect her and their child. He loved Marli, there was doubt in her mind about that. But the one thing he hadn't promised to do was to love *her*.

Harper rose from the sofa. ''Night, Jack,' she whispered, and then quietly left the room.

They arrived in Paris two days later by private jet. Harper was touched that Jack had gone to such expense to protect Marli from being exposed to other travellers in case she picked up a cold. She wasn't old enough for all her vaccinations and his care and concern for her only made it harder for Harper to keep her feelings for him in check. Jack had had to fly back to Rome the morning after the night they'd kissed, which meant there hadn't been time or an opportunity to make love. The anticipation of being intimate with him again sent shivers up and down her spine. Was it her crazy hormones or was it simply because Jack was the only lover to connect with her on such an earth-shattering level?

They were staying at a Livingstone Hotel in Paris which had stunning views of the Eiffel Tower. Jack had organised the delivery of her camera equipment to the hotel and all the baby paraphernalia they needed for Marli. His attention to detail was a comfort to Harper, who was still struggling with see-sawing hormones and lack of sleep—not to mention the experience of being a new mother without the preparation other mothers had.

Harper stood in the penthouse suite in front of

the expansive windows, drinking in the view outside. 'I think Paris is one of my favourite destinations. It's virtually impossible to take a bad photo here. There's something about the light and the architecture. It gets to me every time.'

Jack came up behind her and placed his hands on her shoulders. She could feel the strong wall of his body within an inch of hers, the thrill of his touch sending shockwaves of electricity through her body. She could smell the citrus and woody notes of his aftershave and she could feel her pulse reacting to his proximity with strong, pulsing beats like that of a tribal drum. Beats that reverberated deep in her core.

Jack leaned closer and placed his mouth against the side of her neck, close to her ear. Her skin erupted in shivering sensations and her heartbeat skyrocketed. 'Are you nervous about tomorrow?' he asked in a low, deep burr.

She leaned her head to one side, unable to resist the feel of his lips teasing and tantalising her skin. 'A little, I guess.'

He turned her to face him, his eyes as dark as a midnight sky. 'You'll be brilliant. And I'll take care of Marli, so you don't need to worry about her unless she needs a feed.'

Harper placed a hand on his chest, her gaze dipping briefly to his mouth then back to his gaze. 'I don't know what I would have done if you hadn't wanted to be involved in raising her. I love seeing you with her. But it kind of makes me realise what I missed out on by not having a father.'

Jack stroked a gentle hand down the back of her head, his touch soothing and yet sensual too. 'It's his loss, not yours.' His expression became rueful and he continued, 'I can't believe I would've missed out on the joy of being a dad if we hadn't got pregnant the way we did. I told myself I never wanted children, never wanted the responsibility of keeping them safe and guiding them through life. But now Marli's here, I couldn't be happier. I wish I didn't have to work so hard so I could be with her more. I don't want to miss a thing.'

'You're everything a girl could ask for in a father.'

'You're doing a pretty fine job of being a mum too.'

There was a long moment of silence. A silence where Jack's gaze moved to her mouth and lingered there for a heart-stopping period. A silence where Harper waited with bated breath for him to close the distance between their mouths, the need in her rising with every passing second.

And then finally, the touchdown. But it was hard to know who had moved first. Harper sighed against the firm press of his lips, opening her mouth to wel-

come the erotic command of his tongue. Shivers
skittered down her spine, and as his tongue played
and danced and duelled with hers a pool of molten
heat formed in her core. Desire leapt like wildfire
in her veins, a throbbing, burning, impatient desire
that was threatening to rage out of control.

Jack's mouth shifted position, his kiss deepen-
ing, sending another scorching wave of longing
through her body. He groaned against her mouth as
if he couldn't get enough of her taste. She groaned
back, pushing herself closer to the hard frame of
his body. One of his hands went to the small of her
back, pressing her towards the jut of his erection.
A frisson of delight shot through her flesh in anticipation of his intimate possession.

'I want you so badly,' Jack groaned.

'Then have me.'

His eyes glittered with desire. 'Are you sure?'

Harper stepped up on tiptoe and swept her tongue
across his lower lip. 'I want you to make love to me.'

He gave a whole-body shudder as if the anticipation was getting to him too. 'God, I love it that
you're so hot for me. That was what was so great
about our first time together. You almost blew the
top of my head off.'

Harper smiled a sultry smile. 'Yes, well, you
were pretty hot for me too, if I recall.'

He pushed her closer against his arousal, his

dark eyes smouldering. 'I couldn't bring myself to make love with anyone else until I saw you again. I was desperate to experience it again. The passion, the energy, the sheer alchemy of being with you.'

His confession thrilled her beyond words. Her intimate encounter with him had tilted her world on its axis. It had terrified her to be so attracted to someone that he had distracted her from the work she loved. But it wasn't just her physical attraction to him that was so terrifying. It was the love she had for him. The love she had pretended she didn't feel. The love she had packed away in a box inside her head marked *Do Not Open*. It had struck her like lightning the first time he kissed her. And each kiss since had only poured accelerant on the flames of her feelings. They whooshed through her every time he looked at her a certain way—the way he was looking at her now, with eyes lustrous with want.

'No one has ever made me feel the way you do,' Harper said. 'Sexually, I mean.' She didn't feel ready to confess her feelings for him. Would she ever? He wouldn't welcome them in the context of their relationship. He had made it abundantly clear he wasn't offering her forever love. He was too cynical and jaded to open his heart to romantic love. And the ironic thing was she had been exactly the same until she met him.

'Ditto,' Jack said, surprising her beyond measure. 'You totally rocked me.'

Harper chewed at the edge of her lower lip, a moment of self-doubt coursing through her. 'But what if it's different now? What if we're not as in tune as we were back then?'

His mouth hovered above hers. 'Let's go for it and see, shall we?'

CHAPTER NINE

JACK'S MOUTH MOVED against Harper's with increasing passion, his tongue mating with hers in an erotic dance that left her breathless with want. One of his hands was still in the small of her back, the other came up to cradle one side of her face. No one had ever kissed her like that before. No one but Jack had held her in such a tender and yet passionate way, as if on some level he cared deeply for her. Was it too much to hope he did? That, like her, he was denying his feelings to keep himself safe from hurt? How could someone kiss her with such finesse and not feel something for her? Or was it just plain and simple rip-roaring lust?

Harper returned his kiss with equal passion, her heartbeat accelerating as her body encountered the rock-hard ridge of his erection. The primal need in her flesh responded with fervent heat, the ache to get even closer driving her wild. She whimpered her longing against his lips, urging him on with the flicker and dart of her tongue against his.

Jack's mouth left hers to blaze a trail of fire along her collarbone and then to just above her breasts. Even though she was still fully clothed, the closeness of his mouth to her breasts made her ache to feel his lips and tongue on them. He pushed her top off her right shoulder, moving his mouth over her uncovered skin. How could a shoulder feel so on fire? A shoulder! But that was the magic of Jack. The wild and wanton magic of his touch that spoke to every cell in her body. Igniting her flesh into an inferno of lust.

Jack moved his mouth to her generous cleavage, his tongue diving between her breasts, sending a shockwave of delight through her body. 'You like that?' he asked in a throaty, raspy voice.

'I love anything you do. You seem to automatically know where all my erogenous zones are.'

He gave a sexily crooked smile. 'I bet I can find a few more if you give me time.'

Harper didn't doubt it for one second. She began to undo the buttons on his casual shirt, desperate to get her hands on his skin. 'We're both wearing too many clothes.'

'Let me help you with that.' He shrugged off his shirt and then peeled her top off her. The rest of their clothes came off until they were both standing naked. His eyes roved over every inch of her body and she fought against the desire to cover her floppy belly and full breasts.

'You're so damn beautiful,' he said with a hitch in his voice. He stroked a gentle hand over the flesh of her belly almost reverently. 'Even more beautiful than before.'

'I don't know about that...'

'I do.' His mouth came down and kissed the upper curve of her left breast, sending a tingle of delight to her toes and back. He circled her tight nipple with his tongue and then moved his mouth to caress the underside of her breast. He moved to her other breast, taking his time exploring the subtle changes in her body. Sensations rippled through her in electrifying waves, heat pooling like lava in her feminine tissues.

Harper stroked her hands down his hair-roughened chest, his muscles as toned and hard as if he were carved from marble. But unlike marble, he was warm to touch. 'You've been seriously working out,' she said, circling one firm pectoral muscle with her index finger.

'It was a good way to work off my sexual frustration.' There was a wry note to his tone and a glint in his eyes. 'Hitting the gym with a vengeance.'

'Instead of hitting on strangers at a wedding?' Her tone was gently teasing.

He gave another sexily slanted smile. 'I noticed you from the first time you aimed your camera at me. I was determined to have you from that moment.'

Harper raised her eyebrows in a mock-haughty manner. 'So I was just a conquest to you? Another notch to mark in your playboy pocketbook?'

His expression became more serious. 'You weren't a trophy to collect. I was genuinely intrigued by you. You were so cool and stand-offish and yet you kept looking at me as if you couldn't help yourself.' He brought his mouth closer to hers once more. 'But then, to be fair, I couldn't stop looking at you either.'

'I noticed that.' She stroked her hand further down his body, her fingers closing around his erection. His expression contorted with pleasure and he gave a deep, guttural groan.

'Let's take this to somewhere more comfortable.'

Jack led her to the bedroom, then he joined her on the bed, his limbs tangling with hers as if they had been making love for years. He stroked a lazy hand up and down the flank of her thigh, sending a host of shivers coursing over her flesh. 'I brought condoms.'

'I hope you've switched brands since the last time.'

Another frown settled between his brows and his stroking movements on her thigh stilled. 'That night really changed both our lives in a big way, but I can't find it in myself to regret the birth of our baby, can you?'

Harper couldn't have loved him more than at that moment. 'No, of course not. She's perfect in every way. It's just…' She lowered her gaze to his stubble-covered chin and continued, 'I hope my lack of preparation during the pregnancy hasn't hurt her in some way. Emotionally, I mean.'

He tipped up her chin to bring her gaze back to his. 'Anyone can see how much you love her. She can sense it, I'm sure. I don't think you need to worry on that score.'

Harper gave a rueful smile. 'I think worrying comes with the parenting territory.'

He smiled in return and resumed stroking her thigh. 'But at least you don't have to worry alone. I'll be with you every step of the way.' His mouth came back down on hers in a long, drugging kiss that drove every doubt and fear out of her mind.

Harper moved against him, urging him to take it to the next level. 'You're taking way too long. I need you right now.'

'I have to put on a condom first.'

She watched him apply a condom and held her breath in anticipation. He came back to her, looking at her with such fervent desire burning in his eyes it ramped up her excitement to fever pitch. He kissed his way down from her breasts to her belly, dipping the tip of his tongue into the shallow cave of her belly button. Shivers coursed through her flesh at his caresses, her heart racing as she anticipated his next move. He moved to her feminine mound, using his lips and tongue to separate her folds. His movements were gentle and slow but no less arousing for that. Tingling sensations turned into ripples and then crashing waves of pleasure. She snatched in a breath and went with it, unable to stop it even if she had wanted to. She couldn't hold back her panting cries of ecstasy and she clutched at his broad shoulders to anchor herself from the tumultuous storm racking her body.

'You certainly haven't lost your technique,' she said, struggling to catch her breath.

Jack moved back up to kiss the side of her neck, his strong, muscular legs tangling with hers. 'I want to be inside you.' His husky groan delighted her senses as much as his mouth teasing the sensitive skin of her neck.

'I want you.' Harper had never said those three little words to any other lover. Or at least said them and truly meant them. But with Jack, the need pummelling through her was so desperately intense, she thought she would die without him bringing her to completion.

Jack positioned himself at her entrance, then

with an earthy groan entered her with a slow thrust that lifted every hair on her head. Her body wrapped around him, welcoming him, and darts of pleasure shot through her flesh. He began to move within her, slow but steady, then gradually building his pace as she breathlessly urged him on. He slipped a hand beneath her bottom to tilt her pelvis to increase the friction where she needed it. She wrapped her legs around him, raising her hips to meet each downward thrust, enjoying the thickness of his body in the slickness of hers.

Jack brought his other hand between their bodies and caressed her most sensitive flesh of all. The tight bud of her clitoris that was connected to an orchid-like network of nerves spread throughout her womanhood. She lifted off within seconds of his expert touch, the sensations ricocheting through her body like an earthquake.

His own release followed hers, the deep, thrusting movements of his body only heightening the delight growing through hers. He tensed for an infinitesimal moment and then pitched forward with a primal-sounding growl of pleasure, his body shaking and shuddering and shivering.

Jack stayed connected to her for a long moment, his breathing rate still hectic, his face buried in her neck. 'So it wasn't a fluke, then.' His lips as he spoke tickled her skin, then he raised himself on his elbows to look down at her. 'You sounded like you had a good time.'

Harper smiled. 'So did you.'

His eyes twinkled. 'It was definitely worth the wait.' He rolled off her to remove the condom but came back to gather her close, tucking her into his side, one of his hands stroking up and down her arm.

'Jack?'

'Mmm?'

Harper turned her head to look at him. 'I hope you're not going to wait another nine months to make love to me again. Actually, it's ten months because Marli is almost five weeks old.'

Jack rolled her over onto her back once more, caging her in with his arms. He gave a slanted smile that sent her heartrate soaring and her blood simmering in her veins. 'Not a chance, sweetheart.' And his mouth came down and set fire to hers.

Jack watched on the sidelines as Harper worked on the photo shoot over the next couple of days. She had been given several sites in Paris to photograph and it meant each full day was a juggle of feeds for Marli and setting up equipment in each location. Then taking the shots, reviewing them and working with the support team in deciding on the ones they wanted to feature. It was exciting to be back doing what she did best, but she was conscious of Marli the whole time. Worrying about her, needing to check on her, wanting to hold her longer than for a quick feed but unable to because of the time pressure she was under. It was a revelation to her of the dilemma most working mothers faced each day. There were so many conflicting needs and tasks to see to and it was nothing short of emotionally and physically exhausting. But it also gave her a sense of gratitude that Jack had put a pause button on his own work commitments to be with her. To support her and take care of Marli so she could concentrate on her work.

The last place to photograph was Jardin du Luxembourg in the Sixth Arrondissement of Paris. The gardens had been started in 1612 by Marie de' Medici, the widow of King Henry IV, for the residence she built—the Luxembourg Palace.

Harper was halfway through the shoot when she caught sight of Jack sitting under a tree with Marli propped up against his bent knees. He was playing with her tiny feet and smiling down at her with such love and devotion in his expression it brought a lump to Harper's throat. She aimed her camera at him and took a round of shots from different angles. He hadn't noticed her, so it gave her a perfect opportunity—the one most photographers loved and aimed for—the natural in the wild shot.

But as she was taking the last photo, Jack turned his head and smiled at her. 'How's it going?'

'Nearly done.' She came closer and knelt down to stroke her finger down Marli's chubby little cheek. 'I caught her smiling up at you.'

'She's got a knockout smile like her mother.'

'I think they might be the best photos I've taken today, perhaps for the entire shoot.'

Jack gathered Marli against his broad chest, stretching out his long legs on the grass. 'I can't wait to see them.' He flashed a glinting smile up at her. 'And I can't wait to get you alone tonight.'

Harper suppressed a tiny shiver of anticipation. She placed a hand on his broad shoulder. 'Thank you for making this as seamless as possible under the circumstances. I would've hated to have forfeited this opportunity to showcase my work.'

He balanced the now sleeping Marli along one arm and placed his other hand on top of Harper's. 'We're in this together, sweetheart. We're a team now.'

Harper looked down at Marli so safe and secure against his body. Was it greedy of her to ask for more than he was prepared to give? He clearly loved his baby girl and he had proved himself to be a steady back-up to Harper, not resenting her career commitments or insisting she put them aside for his. He was supportive, encouraging, and was prepared to provide a home and haven for their little family. And he desired her as much as she desired him. Surely that was enough for now?

Later that night, once Marli was bathed and put down to sleep, Jack came out to where Harper was sitting going through her photos on her digital camera.

'Can I see what you took today?' he asked, sitting beside her and stretching an arm along the back of the sofa next to her shoulders.

'I still have to edit a few but some are all right.' She held the camera so he could see the screen and began to click through the hundreds of photos taken that day.

'You've really captured some interesting angles in those shots,' Jack said, leaning closer, the fragrance of her hair teasing his nostrils.

'This is my favourite.' She clicked through until she came to one of him sitting with Marli.

Even Jack was surprised at the candid shot of himself cradling Marli. The love the image captured in that seemingly unobserved moment was enough to melt any hardened heart. He wondered if his own father had felt the same level of devotion towards him when he was a young baby. Or had the pressure of work and then the slow but steady creep of his father's illness stolen the early joy and turned it into bitter disappointment instead?

'Why are you frowning?' Harper suddenly asked.

Jack quickly rearranged his features into a relaxed smile but he could feel the tug of uneasiness deep inside, a question that needed answering. A problem that needed to be addressed. He had never really questioned whether his father loved him, but neither had he ever felt particularly close to him. The early memories of his childhood were overshadowed by the way his father had changed with his illness, becoming more and more distant and difficult and demanding.

'Sorry. I was just thinking about my own relationship with my father.' He let out a long sigh. 'I'm not sure he was as attached to me as I am to Marli, but then it was a different generation. Men were certainly encouraged to be more involved with their kids but my father was not the sort of man who enjoyed being around little kids all that much. And then, by the time I was a little older, he became unwell. Plus, I went to boarding school pretty young.'

Harper placed a gentle hand on his arm, her touch sending instant warmth through his body. 'How old were you?'

'Six.'

A frown pulled at her forehead, a look of shock in her gaze. *'Six?'*

Jack shrugged one shoulder in a dismissive, it-didn't-do-me-any-harm manner. 'I coped.'

'But you were so terribly young. Were you homesick? Lonely? Did you find it hard settling in and making friends?'

Jack had more or less blocked out those early memories. He was a put-it-behind-you-and-move-on-with-your-life sort of person. He didn't ruminate over things that couldn't be changed. But Harper's concerned questions tapped at the locked and bolted door he had stored those memories behind. Memories of acute sadness, despair and loneliness. A sense of having to grow up way too fast but doing it anyway. A gnawing sense that he was a disappointment to his father, that he wasn't loveable, that he had been sent away so his father could get on with work without the distraction of his presence. He suspected his mother had agreed to it to keep him safe from his father's occasional outbursts of temper. Jack had suppressed his emotions so deep down inside himself he was uncertain he could access them now even if he wanted to. As for feeling them...well, he refused to feel them. Feeling them made them real again, painfully real.

'I settled in relatively quickly,' Jack said. 'I made friends, some of whom are still friends to this day.'

Harper studied him for a long moment, her expression still showing shadows of concern. 'But it must have affected you, being away from home for so long. Didn't you miss your mum?'

Jack gave a lopsided smile. 'I did for a bit but I didn't let her know it. She would have told my father and it wouldn't have gone down well with him. He had gone to the same boarding school, and so had his father, my grandfather.' He gave her shoulder a gentle squeeze with his hand that was resting near her along the back of the sofa. 'Now, enough about my childhood. Show me some more of your photos.'

Harper lifted her camera back up and clicked through some more shots, but every time he glanced at her she was still frowning. Was she thinking of her own childhood? How different and even more difficult than his? At least he had had a father. Harper's had refused to have anything to do with her. Was she worried he would abandon Marli in a similar way? He could not think of a single set of circumstances that would ever see him walk away from his baby girl. He was even finding it difficult to think of walking away from Harper. In the past, he was the one who'd *always* walked away. He never looked back, only forward. But he knew in his bones if he walked away from Harper or she walked away from him, something in him would die, or if not die, be stunted.

But why would she walk away? He had given her everything money could buy and he had promised to protect her and their child going forward. The love thing was something she kept referring to but love hadn't been what they started with, only lust. They both loved their little girl, so what else did they need? Nothing he was prepared to give in any case.

Jack took the camera from her and set it aside. He took one of her hands in his, the other he lifted to her face to smooth away the frown between her eyes. 'Stop worrying about my privileged childhood. It hardly compares to what you've been through.'

'I guess…' Her eyes fell away from his to look at her hand encased in his. Then she lifted her gaze once more. 'We've had such different upbringings. How are we going to be the best parents we can possibly be when there are so many things we don't know about each other?'

'We'll get to know each other once we're married,' Jack said. 'Which reminds me, now that your photo shoot is over, let's decide on a wedding date. That was the deal, remember?'

Harper pulled her hands out of his and stood, her expression clouding over like a brooding sky. 'I need more time before I make such an important decision.'

Jack rose from the sofa, a sense of things slipping out of his control tightening something in his stomach. 'There isn't a whole lot of time. Marli is already five weeks old. Before we know it she'll be a toddler and—'

'And what if you can't handle being around a toddler?'

He frowned. 'What do you mean?'

'Kids are hard work.'

'I know that, but we'll have the resources to get help if we need it.'

'I told you, I don't want a nanny.'

Jack scraped a hand through his hair. 'My mother is willing and able to help out and would get a lot of joy out of doing it.'

'And we both know how well your mother and I get on,' Harper snapped back. 'Marli is going to see it and wonder. And then one day she'll be old enough to ask her own questions, like why doesn't her father love her mother like other parents love each other?'

'Not all parents love each other,' Jack pointed

out. 'Especially a few years down the track when careers and kids and other stresses kill the joy of the honeymoon phase. But because we're not starting at the same place, we can be realistic about how our relationship will work. We both admire each other and desire each other. That's a solid and stable platform to build a workable marriage on.'

'It all sounds good on paper, but we'd have to draw up a prenuptial agreement. I don't want anyone saying I only married you for your money.'

'Fine. We'll get a prenup drawn up. We'll go to the best in London if that will ease your mind,' Jack said. 'Drake Cawthorn is a specialist in them.'

She gave him a searching look. 'You know him personally?'

'Only in passing. Why, do you?'

'He's a friend of Aerin's older brother,' Harper said. 'We've sent a few clients his way. I haven't met him in person but I've heard he's pretty ruthless in making sure his clients get protected if things turn sour.'

Jack knew he should be relieved Harper wanted a prenup drawn up but somehow it suggested she didn't give their marriage much hope for the long-term. *You are hardly a long-term guy*, his conscience reminded him but he pushed the thought aside. He had a baby girl, of course he was committed to her in the long-term, and by default committed to her mother.

Not in love, but one hundred per cent committed.

'I'll give him a call and set up an appointment for when we get back to London,' Jack said.

'Okay.'

Jack suddenly realised how much he wished they weren't going straight back to London. He needed more time with her without the distractions of work. He hated the thought of going back to the hard grind of running his company and not seeing either Harper or Marli for hours on end. He was successful enough to step back a little, not too far but a little. He was too driven and goal-oriented to hand the reins over to someone else. He liked to be in control but that didn't mean he had to be at the helm eighteen hours a day.

Jack came over to her and took her hands once more. He looked into her grey-green eyes and smiled. 'Hey, you. Did I tell you how proud I am of your work? I've watched you over the last couple of days, juggling Marli and your shoot. I can't wait to see the final product. Will there be a book launch?'

'Yes, but it will be a few months down the track.'

He tilted up her chin to keep her gaze meshed with his. 'I have a proposal for you.'

Her eyebrows lifted in a wry manner. 'Not another one?'

He grinned and planted a quick kiss on her mouth. 'How about we stay on a couple of extra days in Paris? I can reshuffle my diary and I'm sure Aerin and Ruby will manage without you.'

'It sounds nice…' Her gaze was focused on his mouth, her voice soft and husky. 'I've been so keyed up about the shoot that I haven't had time to properly enjoy our time here.'

He brought her close against his hardening body. 'You've enjoyed *some* of our time here, haven't you?'

A light blush tinged her cheeks pink and her eyes shone with desire. 'Now that you mention it…' She stepped up on tiptoe and placed her lips against his, lighting a fire in his body that threatened to engulf him. He took control of the kiss, his tongue mating with hers in a dance that sent shivers coursing down his spine. He literally could not get enough of this woman. She turned him on like no other. And her desire for him was equally fervent, thrilling him to the core of his being.

If that wasn't a recipe for a good, strong, workable relationship, he didn't know what was. Love was for the romantics and fairy-tale believers. For the hopefuls and the naïve.

Not for him.

CHAPTER TEN

A COUPLE OF days later, Harper walked arm in arm with Jack along the Champs-Élysées. Marli was asleep in the pram, the sun was shining and the birds were singing, and, while the busy Paris traffic with its mix of sirens and horns was noisy, it didn't spoil the atmosphere for Harper. Her body was still tingling from Jack's superlative lovemaking over the last couple of nights. Jack had been an attentive and surprisingly tender lover but now he was even more so. It was as if something had changed in their relationship, a subtle shift that gave her hope that he was developing feelings for her, even though he had ruled out falling in love with her or anyone. But the love he showed towards Marli was unmistakably solid. He was involved with every aspect of her care apart from feeding. It fuelled Harper's hope that he could open his heart to her too.

They were walking past an art gallery when

Jack stopped to look at the artwork displayed in the window. It was a beautiful watercolour with the softest brushstrokes of exquisite pastel colours depicting a cruise boat heading towards one of the River Seine bridges. The brushstroke style was loose and free and yet still managed to capture so much of the essence and light and energy of Paris.

'Shall we go in?' Harper suggested.

'I thought you wanted to go to the eighteenth-century tea salon further down?'

Harper's stomach gave a loud rumble of hunger. Reading about the delicious patisserie with its world-renowned pastries had whetted her appetite, but something about Jack's wistful expression as he stood in front of the gallery window made her curious. 'I do but I'd like to look at the artwork first.' She peered at the French name on a placard next to the painting. 'Etienne Aubuchon. I think I read something about him a while ago. He's very good, isn't he?'

Jack made a grunting sound of agreement and began pushing the pram again. 'We'd better get that cup of tea before Marli wakes for her next feed.'

Harper continued on by his side, wondering why he hadn't wanted to browse through the gallery. It wasn't as if he couldn't afford any of the artworks inside. Perhaps he was one of those people who didn't get the subtlety of modern art, although that painting style leaned more towards Impressionism than modern. They finally came to the quaint tea salon with its array of delectable goodies on show. They were soon seated at a table inside with their orders taken, and Harper had another chance to observe Jack as they waited for their tea and pastries to arrive. Well, *her* pastries, that was.

'Don't you have a sweet tooth, Jack?'

'No.' His lips curved in a teasing and yet indulgent smile. 'But apparently you do.'

Harper rolled her eyes. 'I have a whole mouth full of them, more's the pity.' She gave him a self-deprecating smile and continued, 'I spent years eating my feelings. It took me a long time to realise that no amount of yummy food was going to satisfy the emotional hunger I was feeling. I had to address the source of that hunger.'

A frown pulled at his brow. 'And were you successful?'

She shrugged one shoulder. 'Yes and no. I guess there will always be a part of me that hungers for things I can't have.'

There was a loaded silence.

'You're not the only one who hungers for things they can't have,' Jack said at last, his mouth twisted in a rueful manner.

'What do you still hunger for?'

'Apart from you, you mean?' His playful tone didn't match the shadows in his dark blue eyes, the same shadows she had seen as they stood outside the gallery window earlier.

Harper gave him a mock-scolding look. 'Be serious for a moment.'

There was another silence.

Jack picked up a teaspoon from beside his china cup and saucer even though their tea had yet to arrive. He toyed with the teaspoon like a baton between two of his long, tanned fingers, then he put it down again with a tinkle against the saucer that sounded eerily definitive. His eyes met hers. 'For as long as I can remember I've wanted to be an artist. It was a yearning desire I had to suppress once my father became ill. I knew it was up to me and only me to keep the family business going.'

'Oh, Jack, that must have been so hard.'

'It was at first but, like most things, the pain goes away after a time.'

'But does it really? I mean, you looked so wistful when we were looking at Etienne Aubuchon's work. Is that what you wanted? To be a successful watercolour artist?'

'Finding success is a bit of a lottery in the arts world,' he said. 'I had some talent, but it didn't get the chance to grow and mature. But that's okay. Not everyone achieves their childhood dream.'

'Do you still paint? I mean, in your spare time, as a hobby?'

His lips curved in a wry smile. 'Hasn't anyone told you a workaholic has no spare time?'

Harper frowned. 'And yet you've given up so much of your time to be with us.' She glanced at their sleeping baby in the pram beside their table. 'I can't thank you enough for being so good about everything. It's not been an easy few weeks.'

Jack reached for her hand across the table, his fingers warm and strong around hers. 'Harder for you than for me, I think. You're a wonderful mother, sweetie. I love seeing you with Marli. No one would ever guess you hadn't prepared for her arrival like other mothers. You're a natural.'

'I don't know about that...' Harper looked down at their joined hands. Her engagement ring winked at her as brightly as the sun outside, reminding her of the purpose of this extra time in Paris. Jack wanted a final commitment from her. He wanted a date to be set for their wedding. But how could she agree to a wedding date when he wasn't in love with her? Wouldn't she be setting herself up for more agonising emotional hunger?

'You're too hard on yourself,' Jack said.

'Maybe.'

Their tea and pastries arrived at that moment but Harper had lost her appetite for anything sweet. Her appetite was ravenous for love—Jack's love. Not just his physical lovemaking but to hear him say the words that no one had ever said to her apart from her friends. Her mother hadn't been the I-love-you type, although Harper knew her mother had loved her. Poor Ruby did not have the same assurance from her mother but at least she had won the heart of Lucas Rothwell. No one could ever question his love for Ruby. It shone from his eyes, it vibrated in the air, it charged the atmosphere whenever he and Ruby were together.

Harper wanted the same from Jack, but was her dream too impossible, too far out of reach?

Jack woke during the night to find Harper wasn't beside him in the bed. His heart gave a stutter but then he remembered she was probably up feeding Marli. But in that second or two of panic, it was like reliving the moment all those months ago, finding his bed empty with only the indentation of her head on the pillow to show she had even been there. He flung off the covers and padded out of the bedroom to find Harper gently putting Marli back in the pram in the sitting room.

'I'm sorry I slept through her waking for a feed,' Jack said in a whisper so as not to wake the baby.

Harper turned and smiled at him. 'It's okay. You looked pretty done in.'

He rubbed a hand over his stubble. 'Yes, well, who knew being a tourist was so exhausting?'

She came over to him and placed a hand on his naked chest, and a lightning bolt of lust zigzagged through his body. 'Was it sightseeing or making love until the wee hours?'

Jack shuddered as he recalled the passion they had shared. It never got any less exciting, any less thrilling and mind-blowing. Even juggling the needs of their baby girl didn't seem to kill or even dampen their desire for each other. Didn't that prove they had what it took for a great marriage going forward?

He placed his hands on her waist and brought her towards his body, another shudder going through him as her soft curves met his harder planes and angles. 'I never get tired of making love with you.'

She looked up into his eyes, her lower body pressed closely to his, her hands snaking around his neck. 'What's the longest period you've made love to the same person?' Her question was casually delivered and yet he sensed in her tone a deeper probe of interest.

'Two weeks,' Jack said. 'But that was years and years ago.'

Harper's brows lifted. 'Why so long?'

For some strange reason he didn't want to smile at her dry humour. For he suddenly realised he had never really ventured out of the shallow waters of casual dating. Not until he'd met Harper. Now he was in deep, so deep his feet couldn't touch the bottom. He didn't even know where the bottom was. All he knew was he was not going to swim away from his baby girl. He was not going to abandon Harper, either.

'I had a fling with a woman I met when I was in New York,' Jack said. 'I'm not proud of it, looking back. I didn't know she was married. She conveniently forgot to mention it.'

'Were you in love with her?'

'No, but it rankled that she hadn't been honest with me.'

Harper lowered her gaze to his mouth for a moment. 'So, telling the truth is a standard you uphold at all times?' Her eyes came back to meet his in an almost defiant manner. 'And one you expect in return?'

'There are probably times when a little white lie is okay in order to keep from hurting someone unnecessarily, but I try to be straight with people. I don't promise things I can't deliver. I don't say words I don't mean.'

Harper gave a crooked smile that didn't meet

her eyes. 'Good to know. I would hate for you to pretend to feel things you don't feel.'

Jack placed his hand along the side of her face, gently tilting her head up so her mouth was within reach. 'What I feel right now is almost indescribable.'

'But you don't love me.' Her tone had a sound of resignation about it that plucked at his conscience like a plectrum.

His hand fell away from her face and she stepped back only slightly, but the gap suddenly felt like the width of the River Seine that ran outside their suite below. How could he close it without compromising himself? Without falling in the deep end without any way of getting out? 'You know I care about you, Harper. That's all I can offer you. Care and support and security. You'll want for nothing in life. I'll make sure of it.'

Her eyes misted over, and an invisible hand clutched at his guts. Her expression heralded a warning that he wasn't ready to hear. 'Yes, you'll give me everything but the one thing I want most of all. The thing I've wanted all my life and never got.'

Jack moved a little distance away, determined to stay cool and calm, but it took more self-control than he realised. Fear clawed at his insides, prickly, cold fear that Harper was not going to fall in with his plans for their future. How could he convince her? He had promised her everything he was capable of giving.

He rubbed a hand down his face and released a ragged sigh. 'I don't want to lie to you.'

'It's not me you're lying to, Jack. It's yourself. You're capable of loving and loving deeply. Look at the way you've bonded with Marli. But you don't want to step beyond your comfort zone with me. I get it. I know I'm hardly what anyone would call in your circles a prize catch. But I want to be loved and I can't marry you or anyone without it.'

'I wish you wouldn't run yourself down like that,' Jack said, fighting anger and frustration and fear. 'You're everything a man could want in a partner.'

'But you don't really want a partner. You want a mother for your baby and a lover for your bed. And those roles are not necessarily mutually exclusive. You don't want a soulmate, someone who shares everything with you and you with them. Someone with whom you can be yourself, your *true* self. The person you could be if you would only allow it.'

'You know, you're really losing me with all this psychobabble crap,' Jack said. 'I am who I am. I've been honest with you from the get-go.'

'Yes, you have, and I'm now being totally honest with you.' Harper pulled the ring off her finger and handed it to him. 'I can't marry you, Jack. I'm sorry.' There was a light of determination in her eyes that struck a chord of disquiet in him. She was the only woman to say no to him and it hurt. It hurt in places he had never hurt before. A pain that travelled through his body like a search-and-destroy missile, looking for all the vulnerable corners and crevices he normally kept hidden.

Jack ignored the engagement ring sitting in the middle of her palm. 'Do you need more time? We've only had just over a month together and, what with taking care of Marli and your shoot and—'

'And how much more time would I waste waiting for you to feel something you have decided you can't or won't feel? Weeks? Months? Years of my life?' Harper said. 'I want the fairy tale, Jack. I didn't think I did until…until I met you.'

'But you refused to see me again.'

She gave a gust of a sigh and placed the engagement ring on the coffee table near the sofa. 'Yes, well, you're the only one who is good at lying to yourself. I told myself I disliked you but really it was the opposite I was feeling. You threatened to distract me from my goals and it terrified me. I think that is also why I didn't recognise I was pregnant, even though my symptoms were a little ambiguous. I just couldn't go there in my mind.'

Jack was frowning so hard it was giving him a headache. A band of pain wrapped itself around his forehead, around his neck, around his chest, squeezing, compressing, crushing so he could barely take a breath. He didn't want to hurt her, but how could he promise something he didn't feel? It would only hurt her more in the end. 'Are you saying you love me?'

Harper met his gaze with a level stare. 'I know you don't want to hear it, not from me or from anybody for that matter. But I do love you. I can't say I wanted to fall in love with you but it happened anyway. But I can't be with you if you don't feel the same. I saw what happened to my mother when she loved a man with all of her being but he didn't return those feelings. It destroyed her.'

Jack wasn't sure how to handle what she had told him. Love was a four-letter word he avoided. He avoided it like a deadly contagion that threatened his very existence. He wore an emotion-resistant mask, he wore a suit of armour that was impene- trable. And yet…and yet…he was feeling such ag- onising pain now. Pain that Harper was not going to marry him. She was not going to live with him and bring up Marli with him in the family life he had envisaged.

'So, this is your final decision?' His brusque tone gave no clue to what he was actually feeling. But then, he wasn't sure what exactly he was feeling other than anger, despair, fear and something else that lurked in the background shadows of his mind.

'Yes, Jack, it's my final decision,' Harper said. 'When we return to London tomorrow, I'm moving back to my flat until I find somewhere a little more suitable to live.'

He swallowed a tight stricture in his throat. 'But the house I bought will be available soon. It just needs some more work before it's ready.'

She gave a sad smile that cast her features into shadows like a dimmer switch on a once bright light. 'It's very generous of you but I can find my own accommodation.' She paused for a moment and then continued, 'I find it so odd you're prepared to commit to buying a house and yet you can't commit yourself emotionally. Why is that?'

Jack knew exactly why he was unable to commit. He had never talked about it with anyone before. It was too deeply personal and painful. But he had already shared with Harper his lost dreams of being an artist. Why not share this too? 'I saw what loving my father did to my mother. I know you don't like her that much but she is a good person at heart. She loved my father dearly and was one hundred per cent committed to him in sickness and in health. Unfortunately, my father's illness meant she spent a lot more time dealing with sickness than with health. She gave up all her own aspirations to be by his side, but I'm not sure he ever appreciated her the way she deserved to be appreciated.'

'But he loved her, didn't he? Or did he ask her to have a loveless marriage the way you proposed to me?'

Jack was uncomfortable being compared to his father, especially now he was a father himself. 'I'm not sure if he loved her the way she loved him. Their relationship always seemed a little one-sided. He wasn't a particularly demonstrative man and I don't recall him ever telling her he loved her. He may have done so in private.'

'Did he tell you he loved you?'

'No, but I didn't feel unloved, or at least not in the early days. After he became ill, he changed. He became hard to be around. Only my mother could handle his moods.' And Jack hadn't even bothered trying. Had he missed an opportunity to build a better relationship with his ailing father? It was too late now.

Way too late.

'When will I see Marli?' Jack was aware of his gut tightening into knots. Aware of a sense of dread filling his chest, a creeping fear that he was going to fail as a father because he couldn't be with his daughter the way he wanted to be. He had never planned to be a father but, now that he was, the last thing he wanted to be was a part-time one. But how could he be anything but part-time when Harper wouldn't marry him?

'You can see her whenever you want. I won't stop you. I'll have to think about some day care for her. I need to get back to work at some point.'

'I can do a four-day week or even a three-day one,' Jack said, wondering if he was turning into someone he couldn't recognise. Where was the man who rarely took a weekend off? Where was the man who worked eighteen-hour days? 'And my mother will be happy to help out.'

'I'll think about it.'

There was a silence so intense Jack was sure she would be able to hear each and every one of his hammering heartbeats.

'Of course, it goes without saying that I won't be sharing that bed with you again tonight or ever,' Harper said. 'It's almost morning anyway.'

It hit him then like a punch. The knockout blow of reality that he would no longer hold Harper in his arms. No longer feel her electrifying touch gliding along his skin. No longer feel the soft but passionate press of her lips against his own. She was drawing a line underneath their relationship. A boundary line that he would not be able to cross.

Or at least not without compromising himself in a way he had sworn never to do.

'This…decision of yours seems rather sudden,' Jack said, unable or unwilling to take the bite out of his tone. 'Or did you want to have the extra time in Paris first?'

A hard light came into her eyes. 'It was your idea to extend our stay, for what reason I'm not sure. Did you think it would charm me into agreeing to marry you?'

'It clearly didn't work if it was.'

Harper let out another heavy sigh. 'I don't want any animosity between us, Jack. We have to put our daughter first, and getting on with each other is important.'

He didn't want to *get on* with her. He didn't want some formal, hands-off type of friendship. He wanted *her*. But how could he have her without pretending to feel things he didn't feel?

Jack walked over to the windows but for the first time ever the view did nothing for him. It was just another river winding through yet another city. Paris, the city of love, the most romantic city in the world, was tarnished by his break-up with Harper.

'Jack?'

Jack turned around to face her but he kept his expression masked. 'Let's not drag this out any more. You've made your decision and I've accepted it.' He hadn't but he would force himself to. He was not going to beg her to stay with him. He already had acted out of character by waiting for nine long months for her to contact him again.

'I just wanted to say thank you again for being so supportive. Not many men would have coped as well as you did with the news of a baby arriving so suddenly. You're a wonderful father to Marli. I wouldn't want any of our baggage to get in the way of your relationship with her.'

Jack went over to the pram where Marli was still sleeping soundly. He stroked a barely touching finger over the peachy skin of her tiny cheek and his heart contracted at the thought of not seeing her every day. How would he bear it? How could he have gone from worldly playboy to devoted dad so seamlessly? One thing he knew for sure—he couldn't go back to his old style of living. The footloose and fancy-free lifestyle that had a stream of nameless women coming and going in his life. But neither could he have Harper, the only woman he wanted right now. He was stuck between the two worlds and, unlike along the silvery river outside, there were no bridges.

No safe passage could get him across.

CHAPTER ELEVEN

HARPER FOUND IT sadly fitting that Marli cried on and off for most of the journey back to London. It seemed as if her baby girl was crying the tears she herself was unwilling to shed—or at least not in front of Jack. She had bared her soul to him last night and it had not produced the results she had hoped for. He remained mostly silent on the flight. He helped soothe Marli, which was a blessing because Harper found it difficult to manage those piteous cries when her own heart was breaking.

Finally, the hellish journey was over and Marli was asleep in her capsule as Jack brought it inside Harper's flat. He had arranged for his staff to transport all the baby paraphernalia from his hotel suite to her flat before they got home. He had even organised fresh food to be delivered so she didn't have to negotiate the shops with a young baby. It was another reminder of the power and efficiency at Jack's fingertips—he could get things done in half a day that would take other people a week, if not more.

That he was angry at her final decision was unmistakable. He masked it well with well-bred solicitousness and cool politeness but she could sense it all the same. A brooding frown had barely left his features, his mouth was tight and his eyes had lost their glinting spark. It was his male pride that was hurt but he would have to suck it up. He was used to getting his own way, but this time she couldn't agree to a loveless marriage. Not without compromising or losing part of herself. The part of herself that had craved love all her life. She had finally come to a place where she realised she had to put herself first in order to guarantee Marli's happiness. How could she be the mother she wanted to be if she was in a loveless relationship with her baby's father? Marli deserved better, Harper deserved better…and didn't Jack? How could he be the man he had the potential to be if she fell in with his emotion-free marriage?

Harper watched as Jack glanced around her flat with a critical eye. Was it her imagination or had those paint cracks grown bigger in the past few weeks? And was the leaking tap in the kitchen even louder than before? The carpet was almost bald in one spot. How had she not noticed that before? But work had always been her top priority.

She spent more time at her office than at home, so the flat was somewhere to sleep at night, and because it was only a rental she hadn't bothered freshening it up.

'I know what you're thinking,' Harper said, sinking her teeth into her lower lip.

Jack turned from inspecting the room. 'You have no freaking idea of what I'm thinking.' His tone was bitter, his expression as hard as stone.

She put up her chin, refusing to be drawn into all-out war with him. 'I'm not going to fight with you. We need to be friends.'

His top lip curled. 'You want me to kiss you on the cheek or shake hands whenever we meet? Seriously? After what we had together?' His dark blue eyes flashed like vivid lightning.

Harper could feel a hot blush stealing over her cheeks. She could feel the magnetic pull of him even now, but she knew she had to resist. She had to suppress her desire for him no matter what. She didn't want to be his casual lover. She didn't want to be anything but the love of his life. 'We don't have to kiss or touch at all. We just need to be civil and polite—especially in front of Marli.'

He raked a hand through his hair, leaving it all tousled so that one thick lock fell over his forehead. 'I can't see you without…' He let out a barely audible curse and clamped his lips tightly together.

'Without what?'

His eyes met hers and something tingled in her lower body as if he had sent an electric current across the room. 'You know what.' His voice had a deep and husky edge that unravelled her self-control like a ball of string flung down a steep flight of stairs.

But Harper was made of sterner stuff now she had become a mother. She had made her decision and she was sticking with it. There was no going back. 'I'm sorry, Jack. But that's not going to happen. I can't regret our time together because we have Marli. But I know I will regret continuing a relationship with you that is based on lust, not love.'

He gave a cynical smile that didn't reach his eyes. His eyes, those beautiful, sapphire-blue eyes, were as hard as diamonds. 'I'll see myself out. Call me if you need anything. We'll arrange a visiting schedule once I sort out my diary. It might take a day or two.'

'That's fine. Take all the time you need.'

Jack went over to Marli still sleeping in her capsule. He looked down at her for a long moment, his jaw working, his throat moving up and down. Then he bent and kissed her downy head before straightening again. 'Sleep tight, little one.'

Harper steeled herself against the stranglehold

of emotion filling her chest. He loved his baby girl so much. Why couldn't he love *her*?

Aerin and Ruby came over the very same day bearing prepared meals for Harper and more gifts for Marli. Harper had sent both a text informing them of her situation with Jack. She needed the support of her friends right now, it wasn't as if she had a mother or father to go to for emotional support and nurture. But she was also aware of how much extra work she had thrown at her friends by her cryptic pregnancy. Ruby's own wedding was only a few weeks away and Harper had always planned to be the one to do the photographs. How could she support her friend and be a good mother too? It seemed an impossible juggling act, one she had yet to solve.

Aerin swept Harper up in a hug as soon as she came through the door. 'I'm so sorry things didn't work out between you and Jack. You must be so devastated.'

'And then some,' Harper sighed. 'But I have to be strong. I have Marli to consider now. I can't settle for anything less than love.'

'Did you tell him you love him?' Ruby asked.

'Yes, because I remember saying to you that you did the right thing in not telling Lucas you loved him when you broke up with him. But when you got back together, I realised I was wrong. I had to tell Jack. I didn't see the point in holding it in any more. I had to tell him in order to move forward.'

'Are you sure he doesn't love you?' Ruby asked. 'I mean, Lucas pushed me away too until he worked through his issues. Maybe Jack needs a bit of time to process things.'

'But how much time?' Harper said. 'I don't want to waste my life waiting for him to fall in love with me. What if he can't love like that? He can love Marli but he doesn't seem open to the idea of romantic love.'

'I think you're doing the right thing,' Aerin said. 'I wouldn't want to be with a man who didn't love me, who wasn't the perfect match for me.'

'Jack is hardly perfect but he comes pretty close,' Harper said. 'And he's taken to fatherhood so well.'

'Does he tell Marli he loves her?' Ruby asked.

Harper frowned as she thought about it. 'I don't think I've heard him say the words but you'd only have to see him with her to see he does. Look—I'll show you the photos I took of him with her.' She got her camera out of its bag and quickly scrolled through the shots until she got to the one in the Luxembourg Gardens. Seeing that photo sent a wave of sadness through her that threatened to overwhelm her. Jack was such a doting father. Why couldn't he be a doting husband as well?

'Oh, how gorgeous is that?' Aerin said with feeling. 'He looks absolutely smitten.'

'He certainly does,' Ruby said with a thoughtful look on her face.

Harper closed her camera and put in back in the bag and zipped it shut. If only she could pack away her feelings as easily. Out of sight, out of mind, out of reach.

If only.

Jack had planned to take some more time off work so he could be with Marli but, as luck would have it, things went awry with a hotel development in Brussels. There was no one else he could send in his place at such short notice. Packing a bag and travelling from week to week had never been a problem before. He had always enjoyed the change of scene and the kick of excitement at the thought of new casual dating experiences. But now it sickened him to his gut to think of sleeping with anyone but Harper. He couldn't imagine feeling desire for anyone else ever again. Had fatherhood changed him so much?

Had Harper changed him so much?

His hotel suite in London had never felt less like a home. He was almost glad to be leaving it to go to Brussels, but he knew he would have to come back eventually and face the emptiness of the penthouse. It was full of luxury furniture and top-quality furnishings, it had commanding views over London, and he had staff to wait on his every whim. But oh, what he would have given for the sound of his baby daughter stirring in her sleep. Damn it, he would even welcome a full-on crying jag like the one on the journey home.

His staff had followed his instructions to the letter. There was no trace of Harper or Marli in his suite now—no rattles, or pink-beribboned teddy bears or unicorns that played lullabies. Nothing to remind him how much his life had changed.

Jack's phone rang just as he was closing his travel bag. He glanced at the screen and saw it was his mother. He hadn't yet told her of Harper's decision not to marry him. He hadn't wanted to say the words out loud because it hurt too damn much. 'Hi, Mum, I'm just dashing off to the airport. The Brussels development has a few issues to iron out. What's up?'

'Nothing, darling, I just wondered if I could come by and see Marli.'

'You'll have to ask Harper.'

'Can you put her on for me?'

Savage pain seized him in the gut. 'Not at the

moment.' He let out a rough-edged sigh. 'She's moved back to her flat.'

'Why?'

'She's decided she doesn't want to marry me.'

'That girl has rocks in her head turning down a marriage proposal from you.' The indignation in his mother's tone would have amused him on any other day, but not today. 'Do you want me to talk to her?' she added.

'I don't think it would help.'

'I hope she's not going to make it difficult for me to see Marli.' His mother's voice was less indignant now and more despairing. A despair he could relate to. But it wasn't just Marli he wanted to see each day. It was also Harper.

Jack propped his phone against his shoulder and jaw as he zipped up his travel bag. 'I don't think she'll do that. She wants what's best for Marli.'

'But if she wants what's best for Marli, why isn't she marrying you?'

'Because she wants me to be in love with her and I can't do that.'

There was an odd little silence. Odd because his mother rarely if ever left room for a silence.

'Can't or won't?'

Jack removed his phone from its propped position against his shoulder. 'I've never been in love and I don't intend to start now. It seems to me to be a loser's game. You only get hurt in the end.'

'And you're not hurting now?'

'Not particularly.' It was a blatant lie but he didn't want his mother to worry about him. Or interfere and make things worse.

'Jack… I know you found things difficult with your father,' his mother began in a tone he had never heard her use before. 'But he was a good man, a decent man who loved his family. You probably don't remember the good times, you were too young. His diagnosis completely shattered him. The prospect of being disabled terrified him and it locked him down inside himself. He literally changed overnight. I kept trying to reconnect with the man I fell in love with all those years ago.'

A lump had come to Jack's throat that made speaking difficult. 'And did you reconnect with him?'

His mother gave a lengthy sigh. 'Sadly no. But I lived in hope until his very last breath, because that's what true love does. It never gives up hope.'

Jack put his phone down a few minutes later and frowned as he thought about what his mother had told him. She had given up her career and the best years of her life to nurse a grumpy and difficult man who had once loved her but never shown it in any meaningful way since, up to the day he died.

If anything, it only confirmed his stance on re-sisting falling in love. Feeling true love for some-one seemed to him a pretty painful way to live.

And right now, he could do without any more pain.

A week later, Harper was in her office sitting at her computer trying to edit photos from the Paris shoot, but Marli was fussing in the pram even though she had been fed and changed. So this was the juggle working mothers talked about. The ceaseless demands of a small infant and the press-ing demands of deadlines. Jack was still away in Brussels to deal with some sort of development issue at one of his hotels. They had spoken a cou-ple of times on the phone and he had seemed polite but distant in his manner. But when she'd put on the video function for him to see Marli, his face lit up, reminding her of why she had fallen for him in the first place. Who could resist that killer smile? Those midnight-blue eyes? That sensual touch—?

But no, she was *not* to think of his touch. Not now. Not again. He had probably hooked up with someone else by now. Maybe more than one per-son. Her stomach churned at the thought, jealousy streaking through her like a poisoned arrow.

'Waa-waa-waa!' Marli bleated from the pram,

obviously deciding she wasn't going to settle any-time soon.

Aerin popped her head through the door. 'Can I help? Does she need a cuddle from her Aunty Aerin?'

Harper stood and stretched her stiff back. 'Do you mind? I just need half an hour to work on these photos.'

Aerin came into the room and swept Marli up in her arms. 'I can think of nothing I would like better.' She smiled down at the baby. 'How is the cutest little munchkin in London?'

Marli waved her tiny hands in the air and Aerin captured one and kissed each of her little fingers. 'Gosh, I can't wait to have kids one day.' She gave a heartfelt sigh and glanced at Harper. 'Can I talk to you about something? I know you're busy but...'

Harper pushed her chair back from the desk. She had lost her enthusiasm for the project any-way. She had lost her enthusiasm for a lot of things since she had ended things with Jack. 'Of course you can. What's up?'

Aerin sat on one of the velvet chairs opposite Harper's desk and cradled Marli against her chest. 'You know how I always meet up with the girls I went to school with each year just before Christ-mas? Well, one of the girls is moving to Australia with her husband, so we're bringing forward our catch-up to next month instead.'

'Yes, I remember, but didn't you say you haven't enjoyed going the last couple of years?'

Aerin looked down at Marli, who was drifting off to sleep. 'I'm the last one of our group who isn't married or in a long-term relationship.' She looked back up at Harper. 'I can't bear being the only singleton. Everyone always asks me if I'm dating anyone. I always feel like such a pariah. I'll be thirty next birthday. What am I going to do?'

'So don't go. Why torture yourself?'

'I have to go,' Aerin insisted. 'We've always had perfect attendance since we left school.'

'It won't be perfect attendance next year unless your friend flies back from Australia.'

'No, which is why I don't want to wreck the track record this year—our final year of all being together.'

'So, I guess you have to find a partner in a hurry.'

Aerin looked down at the baby again and sighed. 'Yes...'

'Do you have anyone in mind?'

'No.'

Silly question. At last count, Aerin had an eight-point checklist on what she wanted in a partner. No such perfect man existed as far as Harper knew. 'So what will you do? Pay someone to go with you?'

Aerin's head came up and her grey-blue eyes widened. 'You mean…a male *escort*?' She whispered the word in a shocked tone.

'No, not an escort but someone who could be a stand-in.'

'You mean I should convince someone to *pretend* to be my partner?'

'It's just for a couple of hours and it would certainly stop everyone carrying on about you being single. Surely you know someone who would do it for you? What about one of your brother's friends? The hot-shot lawyer one—Drake Cawthorn.'

A vivid blush crept over Aerin's cheeks. 'Oh, I could never ask *him*.'

'Then you'll have to go to the catch-up alone and face the violins.'

Aerin winced as if the thought horrified her and quickly changed the subject. 'Have you heard from Jack?'

'Yes, he calls every day.'

'How are things between you? The same?'

'The same.'

Aerin gave another sigh. 'I still think you did the right thing. I know Ruby doesn't agree with me but you have to be sure he loves you. How could you build a future on anything less than true love?'

How indeed?

Jack walked through the house he had bought before Harper had called time on their relationship. It had been repainted and recarpeted throughout and the interior designer was in the process of organising curtains and other soft furnishings. The house still needed a bit of work but it was taking shape. What a pity he wouldn't be needing it after all. Or should he keep it so Marli had somewhere to grow up rather than in a hotel? But the house was too big for a single dad and an only child.

A single dad.

How those words were like a punch to the guts. He had planned to be married to Harper by now but she had refused to accept his offer of a secure future. He had been so confident she would fit in with his plans…well, reasonably confident. Harper wasn't the sort of person who could be forced to do things she didn't want to do, which was one of the things he admired about her. One of the many things. Things that made it hard for him to get through a day without thinking of her, without missing her, without wanting her. And the nights were worse, way worse. He had turned in bed several times to reach for her, only to feel the crushing blow of realisation that the other side of his bed was empty.

Harper was gone and she was not coming back.

And somehow he would have to get used to it.

CHAPTER TWELVE

HARPER WAS AT home a couple of days later with Marli when the doorbell rang. She wasn't expecting Jack back until the end of the week and she knew Aerin and Ruby had other commitments. Poor Ruby had even mentioned postponing her own wedding so they could keep up with everything. She and Aerin had taken on so much extra work because of her taking maternity leave, something that worried her deeply. It wasn't just her who had been blindsided by the arrival of Marli but her business partners too. But how could she leave her baby in the care of strangers in order to get back to work? And did she even want to go back to full-time work? She was enjoying being a mother, far more than she'd ever expected to. It wasn't always easy—Marli had occasional colic and it was harder to get her into a routine than all the baby books and parenting blogs said. But Harper loved seeing her grow and her heart melted every time Marli smiled or cooed at her. She was so like Jack in colouring, with those big blue eyes and ink-black hair.

Harper juggled Marli along one of her arms and checked the security monitor Jack had insisted on installing a few days ago. Jack's mother was standing outside with a basket balanced on one arm. Harper opened the door even though she could have done without an impromptu visitor right then, especially one as critical and judgemental as Liz Livingstone. It was four in the afternoon and Harper hadn't had a shower, for Marli had been fractious for most of the day.

'Is it a good time to call in? I know you must be busy with the wee one,' Liz said.

Harper shrugged as if she didn't care either way. 'It's fine. Come in. Sorry the place is a bit of a mess. Marli's not had a decent sleep all day and…' She had to stop before her emotions got the better of her. The last thing she wanted to do was burst into floods of tears in front of Jack's mother.

'Are you okay, dear?' Liz's softer maternal tone only made it harder for Harper to keep control. 'Here, let me take her for you.' She put the basket on the floor and reached for the baby.

Harper handed Marli to her grandmother, her eyes misting over, her chin developing a distinct wobble. 'I'm okay. Just a bit tired.'

Liz rocked from side to side, her hand gently stroking Marli's back in a rhythmic fashion. 'But of course you'd be tired. Looking after a baby on your own is hard work. And the lack of sleep really gets to you. I remember being an emotional wreck most days until I got Jack into a routine.'

'Was he a difficult baby?'

Liz gave a wistful smile and glanced at the baby now settling in her arms. 'Not really. I was the problem, to be honest. I wanted to be the best mother in the world. I set unrealistic expectations for myself.' She sighed and continued in a reflective tone, 'I was missing my work but I felt guilty about it. I thought I should've been happier being a full-time mother like my own mother and my mother-in-law. But I was so *bored* a lot of the time. Of course, I couldn't talk to anyone about it. All of my mum friends seemed happy being at home all day with a baby, but I nearly went out of my mind.'

'I think I have the same problem,' Harper said, only realising it at that moment. The older woman's honesty about her experience had helped Harper to gain more insight into her own see-sawing emotions and increasing stabs of guilt. 'I'm not used to spending so much time at home. I'm usually flat out with my photography, if not taking photos, then editing and formatting and consulting with clients. I want to be a good mother but I also want

my career, and I don't know how to manage both.'
Tears began to leak from her eyes and her shoulders shook with the effort of trying to keep control.

'Oh, you poor darling,' Liz said, patting one of her shoulders in a soothing manner, whilst still managing to settle Marli. 'And you'll be missing Jack, I expect.'

Harper stretched her mouth into a don't-feel-sorry-for-me grimace. 'I'm the one who broke things off.'

'Yes, but I think you did the right thing.'

'Because you would prefer someone a little more acceptable as your future daughter-in-law?' Harper couldn't quite remove the cutting edge to her tone.

Liz gave a hefty sigh. 'I probably deserve that. But I was so shocked when Jack said he was getting married to someone he didn't love. Every mother wants the best for their child and I'm no different. But I worry it's because of me that he resists falling in love.'

'How could it be your fault?'

Liz gave a sad-looking smile and laid the now sleeping Marli in the bassinet. She turned to look at Harper. 'I loved Jack's father so much and we were happy in the early days, but then he got sick and...and well, I lost the man I fell in love with. I nursed him for years, always hoping he would come back to me, but he didn't. I think Jack was deeply affected by that. It made him feel I had given away too much of myself and got nothing in return. But I don't see it that way. I loved my husband, and I took my wedding vows seriously—in sickness and in health, for richer, for poorer, till death do us part.' Her voice trembled on her last sentence but she continued stoically, 'If you love someone with your whole heart and soul, then you love them for ever. I may have lost the man I loved to illness but I didn't lose him, not really. I still have those precious memories of our first years to look back on. No one can ever take that away from me.'

Harper didn't bother hiding her own emotions now. Tears rolled down her cheeks and she stepped closer to hug the older woman. Liz's arms came around her and held her the way a mother would do an adult daughter.

'If you love my son like that, then you're the perfect person for him.'

Harper stepped out of the older woman's embrace and tried to smile, but it fell short of the mark. 'I want to do the best for Marli but I can't marry Jack unless he loves me. I just can't.'

'And you shouldn't,' Liz said. 'You deserve to be loved—everyone does. I wish I could say Jack might change but I'm reluctant to give you false hope. But he is a good person, a loyal and hard-working man who has sacrificed a lot for his family. You've blessed him with a beautiful daughter. Maybe by loving Marli he will learn to open his heart to you.'

'Maybe…'

Liz gave her another warm hug and then released her and smiled. 'Let me help you with Marli. I can babysit while you work. I think I might make a better grandmother than I was a mother.'

Harper smiled in return. 'I would love that. It will be nice for Marli to spend time with you. And it will help me not feel so guilty about letting my business partners down during our busiest season. Marli's arrival blindsided them as well as me and Jack.'

'Well, that's settled, then.' Liz picked up the basket off the floor. 'I brought you a meal and a teddy bear Jack used to have as a baby. I hope you don't mind? I washed it and sewed on new eyes.'

'Of course I don't mind,' Harper said. 'What a lovely thing to do.'

Liz handed her a tattered old teddy bear with only one ear. 'I'm afraid our dog Chester chewed off poor Ted's ear when he was a puppy. But I couldn't bring myself to throw him away.' She gave a self-effacing grimace and added, 'I'm a bit sentimental that way.'

Harper held the old bear against her chest. 'There's nothing wrong with being sentimental.'

'Well, then, I'd better leave you in peace…'

'Why don't you stay and share the meal with me?' Harper said.

'Are you sure?'

'Of course, but if you could mind Marli while I have a quick shower first, I'd be so grateful.'

Liz beamed. 'I would be thrilled to do that.'

Jack finally solved the problem at his Brussels hotel and was at the airport when his flight was delayed by a couple of hours. He cursed himself for not using a private jet but he was trying to do his bit for the environment. He hated killing time, especially now as he was desperate to get back to see his baby girl.

And equally desperate to see Harper.

Only the day before he had stumbled across an olde-worlde toy shop and happened to come across a teddy bear that played the lullaby Harper had mentioned was played by the teddy she had lost in foster care. He wasn't sure why he was buying it for her rather than for Marli. It was kind of like the London house—it seemed the right thing to do. Her childhood had been so lonely and miserable and he had hoped to make her life with him more than make up for the heartache she had experienced growing up. But he was unable to do that now because she'd refused to accept his offer of marriage.

Jack decided waiting around a crowded airport where all he could see was couples and young families was a form of torture. He'd never used to notice kids in prams or babies in front carrier pouches when he was in transit before, but now they were everywhere he looked, striking a deep pang in his heart. And then there were the loved-up couples walking around hand in hand, or greeting each other with deep affection. There was even an older couple who were walking along arm in arm, the old man making sure his frail wife didn't trip on luggage as they made their way along the line to the check-in counter.

Jack hadn't been able to stop thinking about his conversation with his mother a few days ago. Love had always seemed to him a terribly painful exercise, one he didn't want any part of. There were too many sacrifices to make, too much freedom to be lost, too much distress if the love wasn't returned or was blighted by illness as in his father's case. The dementia component of his father's Parkinson's Disease had taken away the man Jack's mother had loved, and yet she had willingly kept loving him and nursing him till his death. She *still* loved him.

What would it be like to be loved like that?

To be loved so deeply you always knew the person had your back? You always could rely on them to want the best for you. That nothing would destroy the commitment they had made to you.

Jack glanced back at the older couple who had now checked in and were walking towards the security checkpoint. The old woman smiled at her husband and the old man smiled back. Their faces were lined with age and their bodies not anywhere near as vital as they had probably once been, but the love they had for each other was there for all to see. A love that would get them through the winter years of their marriage and beyond…beyond to the scary unknown.

Jack realised then that, no matter who you loved, there was a risk you would lose them one day. Age, illness, tragedy—there was no way of escaping the pain of loss unless you didn't love in the first place. But what sort of life would that be?

Your life.

The words dropped into his head and he couldn't get them out. He had resisted feeling the way that old couple felt for each other. He had resisted feeling what those young couples felt as they walked hand in hand. He had resisted feeling what his mother felt for his father.

He had resisted his true self, his true nature.

He had shut it down, locked it away so he could keep himself safe. But Harper's coming into his life had changed everything. From their first night together something had shifted in him but he had refused to face it until now.

He was in love with her.

Deeply in love for the first time in his life. That was why it had terrified him so much, that was why he had stubbornly refused to acknowledge it. Harper had told him she loved him and yet he hadn't told her he loved her back. He hadn't said those words to anyone in his life. Not to his father or his mother. And to his eternal shame, not even to his baby girl. What sort of man did that make him? A scared man. A man running from fear. Fear of loss, fear of being hurt, fear of experiencing emotional pain.

But that was about to change.

If only he could get on a damn flight back to London.

Harper was working on an advertisement at her flat for an assistant to help her with her workload. Liz Livingstone had suggested it over dinner the other night and she had finally decided it was the best way forward. Liz was still going to babysit but it would mean Harper wouldn't be too overwhelmed with the pressure of work when she finally got home each day. It was a matter of balance, something Liz had encouraged her to aim for instead of being so all-or-nothing as Liz herself had once been. Harper was enjoying the new-found friendship with Jack's mother, not only because it gave her an insight into Jack and his family life, but also because Liz was becoming like a mother figure to her. Liz was warm and supportive towards Harper and she absolutely adored Marli and loved being a grandmother. And interestingly, Marli had stopped being so unsettled and fractious and seemed to enjoy being cuddled by her grandmother. And as a result, Harper had found it easier to relax as a mother, not trying too hard to do everything perfectly but allowing that some days were better than others and just enjoying each moment for what it was.

The doorbell rang just as Harper was thinking about going to bed. She checked the security camera and saw Jack standing there looking a little travel worn. He was carrying a toy shop bag in one hand. She ignored the leap of her heart, the race of her pulse, the rise of her hopes. He was coming to visit his baby girl, not her.

Harper opened the door and stepped back, barely able to look at him without wanting to throw herself into his arms. 'It's late. Couldn't you have waited until morning to drop by to see Marli? I've not long put her down.' She wasn't proud of the resentful note in her tone but she didn't want to seem too eager to see him. Let him think she was over him. That her love for him had withered and died for lack of encouragement.

Jack stepped over the threshold and closed the door. 'No, it couldn't wait. I had to see you as soon as possible.'

'Me? Why me?'

A crooked smile formed on his lips and the spark she loved so well was back in his dark blue eyes. 'I've missed you so much. I can't believe it has taken me so long to realise this, but I love you.'

Those three little words hung in the air for a long moment because Harper couldn't decide whether he had actually said them or she had imagined he had.

'Pardon?'

His smile widened and he dropped the bag he was holding and reached for her, taking her by the hands and drawing her close. 'My darling girl, I've been such a damn fool. I think I fell in love with you that first night at the Tenterbury wedding. You caught my eye and you captured my heart. I love you with all of my being. I have fought it, resisted it, denied it, but I can do so no longer. I can't be the man I want to be, the man I was meant to be, without you by my side. Will you please think again about becoming my wife? Please?'

Harper stared at him speechlessly, her heart thudding so excitedly in her chest until she was sure her ribcage would be bent out of shape or permanently damaged. 'You're not pretending to be in love with me so I will agree to marry you?'

'No, darling. I was pretending *not* to be in love with you all these months,' Jack said. 'Pretending to you, pretending to my mother, but, most foolishly of all, pretending to myself. I've always thought loving someone was a dangerous thing to do. I watched my mother love my father and it always seemed so one-sided to me. But she has no regrets about that. She was all in from the moment they met and she never stopped loving him, even when his illness changed him. I want to be loved like that. I want to love like that. I *do* love you like that.'

Harper wrapped her arms around his neck and lifted her face to be kissed. 'Kiss me, Jack. Convince me this is really happening.'

Jack placed his mouth on hers and kissed her deeply, holding her so close she could feel every firm plane of his body. A few breathless minutes later, he pulled back to gaze down at her with so much love shining in his eyes it took her breath away. 'No one has ever made me feel the way you do. It's not just about having Marli. I would have fallen in love with you even if she hadn't come along the way she did. It's why I couldn't date anyone else. I didn't want to feel anyone else's touch in case it made me forget yours. I guess that's why my mother has never dated anyone since my father died. I want us to grow old together, to bring up our little family. We will face whatever we have to face together. There are no guarantees that we won't be touched by tragedy or illness, but I promise to be there for you no matter what.'

'Oh, Jack, I can think of nothing I would love more than to be your wife and partner in life,' Harper said. 'I've been hungry for love all my life but, like you, I pretended for so long that I didn't want it because I was protecting myself from disappointment in case I couldn't have it. Meeting you that night at the wedding turned my world upside down, not just because of getting pregnant, because I didn't even realise that had happened. But also because I knew if I allowed myself to fall in love with you, I would be opening myself up to certain heartbreak. You were a playboy. I was a career girl who wanted no complications in my life—I'd had enough of them in my childhood. But I fell in love with you anyway. I couldn't help it.'

Jack kissed her soundly again, his mouth so tender and yet so passionate it made her blood sing in her veins. He lifted his lips off hers and looked down at her with twinkling eyes. 'I was sitting at the airport in Brussels because my flight was delayed. I saw all these loving couples and families walking past—old ones, young ones and everything in between. It really made me think about why I was avoiding love. It made me realise that before you my life was empty of everything but work. My relationships were shallow and temporary and completely transactional. You're the first person I've ever wanted to commit to. You opened my heart, my love, and I can't thank you enough.'

Harper's heart was so full of joy she could barely speak. She placed her hand on the side of his stubbly face and gazed into the midnight-blue of his eyes. 'My love for you is so deep and all-consuming it will take me a lifetime to show you.'

He smiled down at her. 'A lifetime sounds good.' He bent down and picked up the toy shop bag. 'I bought this for you in Brussels.'

Harper took the bag from him and pulled out a teddy bear. 'I thought that must've been for Marli.'

'No, it's for you to replace the one you lost.'

Harper turned the bear over and found a gold key in its back. She turned it a few times and the sweet cadences of her favourite lullaby filled the air and filled her heart with even more love for this sensitive man who had made her dreams come true. 'Oh, Jack, it's so sweet of you. I missed that bear for years.'

He gathered her close again, the bear crushed between them. 'I missed you more than I can say. I kept searching for you in my sleep, only to wake up bitterly disappointed.'

She gazed up at him. 'I missed you too. So very much.'

'I was at the London house the other day,' Jack said with a crooked smile. 'It's like me—it still needs a bit of work, but I think it will be fine in the end.'

'I can't wait to see it. I've never lived in a proper house before.' She stroked the length of his strong nose and added, 'I have a confession to make.'

'What?'

Harper smiled. 'I've fallen a little bit in love with your mother as well.'

'Have you really?'

'She's been amazing while you've been away. She's going to help me with Marli so I can get back to work part-time. I feel comfortable leaving Marli with her because she loves her so much.'

'Oh, my darling, I'm so glad,' Jack said. 'That's such wonderful news.'

'Jack…will you promise me something?'

'Anything, my darling.'

'Will you promise to paint me a picture? I would

love to be the first person to own a Jack Living-stone watercolour.'

His eyes lit up and a wide smile spread across his face. 'It's a deal. I'll bring some brushes and paints on our honeymoon. Who knows what fun that could be?'

'The paints and brushes or the honeymoon?'

'Both.' He bent down to plant a kiss on her lips.

'Waa-waa-waa!' came Marli's piercing cry from the bedroom.

Jack grinned and released Harper. 'I almost forgot I have something to say to our baby girl.' He took her hand and led her to where Marli was wide awake and wailing in her bassinet.

Jack reached down and scooped the baby out, and she immediately stopped crying and blinked up at him with eyes the same colour as his.

'I love you, little one. Your daddy loves you so much.' He smiled at Harper and added, 'And I love your beautiful mummy too, more than words can ever say.'

* * * * *

HARLEQUIN
PRESENTS

#4057 CARRYING HER BOSS'S CHRISTMAS BABY
Billion-Dollar Christmas Confessions
by Natalie Anderson

Violet can't forget the night she shared with a gorgeous stranger. So the arrival of her new boss, Roman, almost has her dropping an armful of festive decorations. *He's* that man. Now she must drop the baby bombshell she discovered only minutes earlier!

#4058 PREGNANT PRINCESS IN MANHATTAN
by Clare Connelly

Escaping her protection detail leads Princess Charlotte to the New York penthouse of sinfully attractive Rocco. But their rebellious night leaves innocent Charlotte pregnant...and with a Christmas proposal she *can't* refuse.

#4059 THE MAID THE GREEK MARRIED
by Jackie Ashenden

Imprisoned on a compound for years, housemaid Rose has no recollection of anything before. So when she learns superrich Ares needs a wife, she proposes a deal: her freedom in exchange for marriage!

#4060 FORBIDDEN TO THE DESERT PRINCE
The Royal Desert Legacy
by Maisey Yates

If the sheikh wants Ariel, his promised bride, fiercely loyal Prince Cairo *will* deliver her. But the forbidden desire between them threatens *everything*. Her plans, his honor and the future of a nation!

#4061 THE CHRISTMAS HE CLAIMED THE SECRETARY
The Outrageous Accardi Brothers
by Caitlin Crews

To avoid an unwanted marriage of convenience, playboy Tiziano needs to manufacture a love affair with secretary Annie. Yet he's wholly unprepared for the wild heat between them—which he *must* attempt to restrain before it devours them both!

#4062 THE TWIN SECRET SHE MUST REVEAL
Scandals of the Le Roux Wedding
by Joss Wood

Thadie has not one but two reminders of those incredible hours in Angus's arms. But unable to contact her twins' elusive father, the society heiress decides she must move on. Until she's caught in a paparazzi frenzy and the security expert who rescues her is Angus himself!

#4063 WEDDING NIGHT WITH THE WRONG BILLIONAIRE
Four Weddings and a Baby
by Dani Collins

When her perfect-on-paper wedding ends in humiliation, Eden flees...with best man Remy! Their families' rivalry makes him *completely* off-limits. But when their attraction is red-hot, would claiming her wedding night with Remy be so very wrong?

#4064 A RING FOR THE SPANIARD'S REVENGE
by Abby Green

For self-made billionaire Vidal, nothing is out of reach. Except exacting revenge on Eva, whose family left a painful mark on his impoverished childhood. Until the now-penniless heiress begs for Vidal's help. He's prepared to agree...*if* she poses as his fiancée!

YOU CAN FIND MORE INFORMATION ON UPCOMING HARLEQUIN TITLES, FREE EXCERPTS AND MORE AT HARLEQUIN.COM.

HPCNMRB1022

Read on for a sneak preview of
Dani Collins's next story for Harlequin Presents,
Wedding Night with the Wrong Billionaire

"It's just us here." The words slipped out of her, impetuous, desperate.

A distant part of her urged her to show some sense. She knew Micah would never forgive her for so much as getting in Remy's car, but they had had something in Paris. It had been interrupted, and the not knowing what could have been had left her with an ache of yearning that had stalled her in some way. If she couldn't have Remy, then it didn't matter who she married. They were all the same because they weren't him.

"No one would know."

"This would only be today. An hour. We couldn't tell anyone. Ever. If Hunter found out—"

"If Micah found out," she echoed with a catch in her voice. "I don't care about any of that, Remy. I really don't."

"After this, it goes back to the way it was, like we didn't even know one another. Is that really what you want?" His face twisted with conflict.

"No," she confessed with a chasm opening in her chest. "But I'll take it."

He closed his eyes, swearing as he fell back against the door with a defeated thump.

"Come here, then."

Don't miss
Wedding Night with the Wrong Billionaire.

Available December 2022 wherever
Harlequin Presents books and ebooks are sold.

Harlequin.com

HARLEQUIN

Heartfelt or thrilling, passionate or uplifting—Harlequin is more than just happily-ever-after.

With twelve different series to choose from and new books available every month, you are sure to find stories that will move you, uplift you, inspire and delight you.

SIGN UP FOR THE HARLEQUIN NEWSLETTER

Be the first to hear about great new reads and exciting offers!

Harlequin.com/newsletters